CAPTURING SOSIMO

A CLEAN ROMANTIC SUSPENSE

SARA BLACKARD

Want to know how it all began? Find out what propelled Zeke and the team to create the Stryker Security Force by signing up for Sara Blackard's newsletter, and you'll receive **Mission Out of Control**, the *Stryker Security Force* prequel for FREE.

www.sarablackard.com

To all my Advanced Readers,
You all make my books the best they can be.
Thanks for being an awesome and supportive team.
I couldn't do this without you!

ONE

June Paxton crossed her suite, chewing on her thumbnail. She liked the apartment-style room at the St. Regis Hotel in Aspen, Colorado. It afforded her the space to walk off her nerves. She spun and marched toward the window, wishing she could go hiking in the jagged mountains instead of talking on the phone with her father.

"Junebug, are you listening to me?" Her father's commanding voice brought her back to attention.

She sighed. "Yes, sir. I'm listening, but I don't think I need to worry like you're saying." She spun back the other way toward the table where her computer sat. She had a million things to do before the charity event in two days and listening to her father harp on her wasn't on her to-do list.

"This is serious, little girl. If you don't take the precautions necessary, I'll come out there and guard you myself." His voice had taken on that tone that one didn't argue with.

June rolled her eyes. Being the daughter of General

Daniel Paxton came with a lot of orders and commands. While she loved her father and knew that he tried to do what he thought best for her, she also figured with her being thirty-one years old and having made a fortune on her own, she didn't need him taking command of her life anymore. If he came to the event, then everyone would know that Reagan MacArthur—entrepreneur, philanthropist, inventor, and the person she'd made up—was actually June Paxton, the general's daughter. She had lived under that shadow long enough. She didn't want it to darken her path now.

"Dad, I already told you, I've hired security. You have nothing to worry about." She clicked her computer on, pulling up her emails as she tried to figure out a way to close this conversation.

"True, you hired security for the event, but you didn't hire any security for yourself. Adam told me about the emails you're getting. That's not something that you should take lightly."

June gritted her teeth and wished that she hadn't called Colonel Adam Johnson, her contact from the Soldier Enhancement Program, or SEP, to tell him she needed to meet with the board earlier than planned due to persistent emails from an unknown entity. She shook her head at her idiotic mental slip. She should have known that he would tell her father. Adam and the general were wonderful friends, after all.

"June, are you listening to me?"

"Yes, Dad, I'm listening."

"Good. I'm sending you the number of a security firm there in Glenwood Springs. These are guys I trust implicitly. Call them. That's an order. I don't want to step in, but if you don't have them come to be your personal guards, I will." Her father sighed on the other end, and her face turned hot with the command. "I still can't believe that you're holding a poker tournament. Do you have to continue to throw everything we taught you aside? I thought I made it clear that there were other ways to make money than that."

June squeezed her eyes shut at another way that she had disappointed her father. When she'd come up with a poker tournament based on the movie *Maverick* for the charity event, she'd thought she'd struck gold. In fact, all the slots for players had filled up within a week, with many prominent conservative Christians being the first on the list. She knew people varied in what they thought was right and wrong. She just wished her father would understand where she was coming from. That they could disagree on issues but still respect one another. Instead, he just continued his form of religious conversion— commands and outright disappointment.

"Dad, we've talked about this before. I don't have to agree with everything you believe. And besides, this den of evil that you're so proud to preach against has raised over twenty-five million dollars for the soldier fund. And with guests like the Christian guys from Duck Dynasty being one of the first to sign up, I don't think I'm throwing my chips in with the devil over this."

"I just wish you weren't so bent on breaking your mother's heart." The general's words sent shards of pain through June's chest.

No matter what she did, she couldn't seem to add up

to what her father expected of her. Her mother supported her quietly in everything she did, while her father seemed bent on finding fault in everything.

"I'm sure she'll get over it. Listen, I gotta go. Send the information, and I'll call your hound dogs. Love you. Bye." June hung up the phone before her father could answer, knowing the action proved childish and rude.

She tossed her phone onto the table, pushed her laptop back, and rested her head down on her arms. Just great. On top of all the stress of the upcoming event, she now felt guilty for the way she had talked to her father. Ugh, why couldn't he at least consider that though she didn't believe every little thing he did, she still was a Christian? She loved and followed Jesus but didn't see the world in black and white like her father did.

She sniffed and rubbed her nose on the back of her hand to relieve the sting in her eyes. Since her brother's death at sixteen, her father's residual fear strangled her with his overprotectiveness. If that hadn't been enough of a reason, being General Paxton's daughter added a whole extra level of control to her life.

Her phone beeped with a text at the same time that her computer pinged, alerting her to a new email message. She grabbed her phone. The brief text made her eyes water.

DAD: Sorry, Junebug. Love you.

He'd attached the contact information for Stryker Security to the text. She sighed. They both loved each other, and since she didn't want to let him down more than she already had, she would give the guard dogs a call. She typed him a quick message, apologizing and promising to call Stryker.

She glanced at her computer, and her heartbeat picked up. Another email had come in from the company hounding her about wanting to purchase her latest invention. Most people would be thrilled with the amount of money they were offering her. At first she'd been ecstatic. However, when she had researched the company and had come up with little information, her warning bells had rung at DEFCON 1 levels.

At first the emails had been professional, but each time she turned them down, the tone had changed a little. When she'd stopped answering them all together, they'd escalated to vaguely veiled threats. She had called Adam to move up her presentation, figuring the sooner she got the design, patent, and contract to the government, the sooner she could tell this mystery company the design no longer belonged to her. She clicked the new email open and read:

From: WPA Investments, Inc.

Date: October 22

We will get your design one way or another. Let's proceed the easy way, Miss MacArthur.

JUNE STOOD with force from the table, toppling her chair to the floor. Pacing to the window, she worried her thumbnail between her teeth again when she ran the words of the email through her mind. Her heart raced in her throat as she peered at the mountains for comfort. When none came, she marched back to the table and snatched up her phone. She and her father might not see eye to eye on everything, but she conceded that his thoughts on this might be right. She tapped on the contact information and, with a scowl, touched the circle phone icon under the Stryker Security business name. Like it or not, it looked like she needed to hire herself a shadow.

SOSIMO RIVAS TURNED the wrench a last twist as he finished working on Samantha Jones's car. He excelled in this kind of work, using his hands and brute force to fix things that were broken. Pulling items destined for the junk heap back to life. He laughed, shaking his head at himself. Fixing cars that belonged in a junkyard was not as poetic as all that. It was a job that needed done and just about the only one he could do well. It was what had made him valuable to his team during his enlistment in the Army as a member of a highly classified Special Ops unit.

"What are we gonna do now?" Evangeline Jones's cute four-year-old face smiled over at him from where she leaned into the engine.

Sosimo chuckled as her forehead furrowed, a grease mark smeared across it. She had more grease covering her freckles on her dark cheeks, and her hands were filthy. Good thing Sam wasn't one of those fussy moms, otherwise he might be in trouble.

He enjoyed having a kid around, something he'd forgotten the last ten years in the Army. Being the middle child of a family of ten kids, there'd always been littler kids around. He'd loved growing up in a chaotic house, even if his brainy siblings had teased him as a gearhead.

"Now, mi buburjita, we see how well we fixed it." He picked her up by the waist and swung around in a wide arc, her fabric fairy wings flapping in the wind, and set her on the ground. Slamming the hood, he grabbed her hand and circled the car to the driver's side.

"Hop on in and turn the key."

Eva's blue eyes sparkled as she looked up at him, an enormous smile pushing her freckled cheeks up into the most adorable look. "I get to start it?"

"Sí, start it up. Póngalo en marcha."

Sosimo had spoken Spanish to Eva since the day she got there. Like any child, she took to it quick, like lightning. How could he be away from his Venezuelan roots for ten years, but the importance of teaching his language to the next generation still burn strong? Would he ever have kids of his own to pass the tradition down to?

Eva climbed onto the ratty seat and pointed to the key in the ignition.

Sosimo nodded his head. "Okay, sweetie, turn the key, and we'll see if we fixed this old car of your mama's."

Eva reached for the key, her face turning serious as she bit her lower lip. The engine roared to life, and she jumped. She laughed, clapping loudly before tossing herself into his arms.

"We did it." Eva squealing in his ear had him wincing. "Lo logramos."

"Sí, buburjita. We did it. Gracias por ayudarme. You're a good helper." He gave her another hug.

Pride shone in her bright blue eyes.

"Sosimo, man, you steal my fairy princess?" Rafe came into the garage, his arms crossed in mock anger.

Eva giggled and laid her head on Sosimo's shoulder.

"You're wrong, Rafe. She's not your fairy princess. She's my little mechanic." He patted her back as she tightened her hug.

"I helped Sosi fix Mama's car. He even let me start it," Eva said to Rafe before turning a blinding smile on him. "I've never, ever gotten to do something as important as that before."

Rafe rubbed the grease spot on her cheek. "My fair Eva, you didn't tell me you were a mechanic fairy princess. You keep getting more special every day." He reached for her and pulled her into his arms. "Come on. Let's go find Tina. Sosi and I have to go do boring work."

"Hasta luego, buburjita. Thanks again for helping." Sosimo waved as Rafe took her up the stairs to her apartment above the garage.

Eva yawned as she looked over Rafe's shoulder back to Sosimo. "Hasta luego, Tio. I love you."

Man, she killed him with her cuteness. "También te amo."

She smiled big as her blue eyes drifted shut. He turned back to the car to put the tools away, rubbing his hand across his heart. If he didn't think Zeke was firmly on his way to falling in love with Eva's mother, Sam, she and Eva might tempt him to see if something more than friendship could develop. The combination of a beautiful woman, who had struggled through life and survived, and a precious daughter had all his family instincts flaring to life. But with it being apparent to everyone but Zeke from the day Sam and Eva moved out here that something smoldered between those two, Sos hadn't even considered Sam as an option.

However, having Sam and Eva around had Sosimo thinking maybe he should get serious about chasing down a wife. His stomach twisted with the thought. He hated dating, hated the false front people put up to impress one another. Hated finding later that the person wasn't who he'd been thinking all along. He'd been told enough lies growing up that the thought of them left a bitter taste in his mouth. Lies from his parents about how smart he was. Lies from his teachers that he'd never amount to anything. Lies from ex-girlfriends that only wanted the status of hooking up with a soldier. He slammed the wrench onto its hook on the organized wall. On second thought, he did all right on his own. No need to put up with false pretenses if he didn't have to.

"Man, she is one cute kid." Rafe stomped down the stairs, running his hand over his perfect hair. He paused, his foot stopping in midair as he glanced at the wall Sosimo hung the tools on, then continued down the stairs. "Dude, you outlined the tools?"

Sos crossed his arms and glared. "Yes. I'm sick of you guys coming in here, stealing my tools, then tossing them on the closest flat surface. Every time I come in here to work on something, my stuff is never where it's supposed to be."

"Okay, okay. Geesh, you're crankier than a four-year-old." Rafe grabbed a socket wrench from Sosimo's work table, flipping it in the air and catching it. "So, you'll probably hate when I take off with this." Rafe dashed out of the garage and across to the main house at a dead run. "Meeting in five," he hollered over his shoulder.

Sosimo dropped his chin to his chest and shook it. Rafe ran the fastest out of all of them, and he knew it. Chasing after him would only give in to Rafe's infantile nature. Sosimo put away the rest of the tools, washed the dirt and grease off of himself, and headed into the house.

He thanked God every day that he got to be a part of this mishmash family. When he got out of the Army, he hadn't known what he would do. He had spent the last ten years of his life protecting the nation in whatever way needed. While he probably could've opened an auto shop back in Florida where his parents lived, he'd find no genuine enjoyment from making a living that way. So when the chance to be part of Stryker Security Force came up, he'd grasped the opportunity tight with both hands. He'd never be as smart as Rafe or a skilled leader like Zeke. Never had been. Yet, he had been keeping people safe since middle school.

Sosimo stomped into the main house and glared at Rafe, who lounged on the couch with a smug look on his face. Sosimo rolled his eyes and crossed to the kitchen. The guys gathered around the table, and the TV showed stats of their next mission.

"So, are you going to tell me where you hid it?" Sosimo grabbed a glass and filled it with water.

Rafe shrugged. "Maybe. Maybe not."

"Just be careful or I might decide I want to take up computer programming." Sos took a deep drink of his water, staring Rafe down across the room.

"You wouldn't dare." Rafe's eyelids closed to a slit.

"Maybe." Sosimo moved into the living room with a smirk and took the empty seat. "Maybe not."

Rafe opened his mouth to say something only to have Zeke cut him off. "All right, pay attention. Our client is Reagan MacArthur, a philanthropist who is heading up a charity event this weekend up in Aspen."

Zeke pushed the button on his remote, and a picture popped up onto the screen of a woman with a hesitant smile and ginger hair cascading down her shoulders. Something about the look on her face clenched Sosimo's gut. The way she slightly pulled her lip between her teeth made her appear vulnerable. He hoped she wouldn't be as pretentious as some of their other clients.

The only unpleasant thing about their new gig was the people they protected. They ranged in different backgrounds and attitudes, and he had noticed that they mostly just pretended their help didn't exist. Not that it really bothered him too much, but the ones that really got him fired up were the ones constantly questioning their security measures, like they were the experts instead of his team. Sosimo hoped she didn't turn out to be like that, otherwise this weekend would be long on top of boring.

"She's been getting some threatening emails lately, and though she isn't fully convinced it's necessary, she's been advised to take on personal security for this event." Zeke clicked to the next slide.

"It's a charity event for Armed Forces?" Derrick leaned forward, and his voice rose.

"Yes, she's an enormous supporter of the military. She's actually the one who invented the Eyes Beyond that we got about three or four years ago." Zeke looked around at them.

They all knew the tech he talked about, a gadget that let them peek through buildings and cars and registered heat signatures and incongruent shapes. It had saved their butts on many missions, giving them intel that would've left them otherwise vulnerable. In one mission, the scanner had registered an inconsistency in a vehicle parked along all the others. It had been an IED. Without that device, they wouldn't have all made it home from that mission. If they would've had it on their worst mission with the Army, the one where they lost Ethan Stryker, the mission probably would have gone down differently. Sosimo shook the troubling memory away, but his summation of their new client increased tenfold. Maybe this weekend wouldn't be all bad.

"Sos, you're taking point on this." Zeke's quick command had Sosimo flexing his fingers, his lungs expanding to their fullest.

Relief tingled his hands. This job seemed to be an easy one. He wasn't ready for something more dangerous. A mission where his decisions could leave someone injured or dead. He peeked over at Jake before nodding and turning his attention back to Zeke.

"This should be a fun weekend for you all." Zeke smirked.

"You're not coming?" Jake rubbed a hand over his scarred cheek, and Sosimo's gut clenched.

"I don't want to leave Sam and Eva here alone just yet." He rubbed his hand over his short dark hair. "Not with the Paynes still causing problems."

They all nodded their agreement. That family definitely lived up to their name. Sosimo focused as Zeke laid
out the weekend. He had to get this right, had to recognize every possible point of weakness. He darted his eyes
again at Jake, his gaze swinging to the leg that now
sported a prosthetic. Sosimo's chest tightened. He
couldn't afford any lack of attention, never again.

TWO

A knock sounded on the suite door, pulling June's attention from her assistant on the phone. Her stomach rumbled in anticipation of what she hoped proved to be a greasy cheeseburger and hot fries.

She had a problem. She knew.

She should have ordered a healthy salad, maybe a fruit tray. The stress of this event proved to affect her the same as when she focused on an invention—forgetting to eat until her stomach rioted with nausea and loud groans of wanting. When she got to that point, all hopes of healthy choices went out the window. She needed meat, lots of it, and fried carbs. She swallowed the drool that pooled in her mouth and hustled to the door, promising her protesting stomach that relief was just a few seconds away.

"Mandy, I'm gonna have to call you back." She opened the door. "I have to shove this burger in my face before I ..."

Her words trailed off as the most gorgeous man she'd

ever laid eyes on stood in front of her, his eyebrow cocking. She'd grown up on Army bases around the world. She knew good-looking when she saw it, and this Latin specimen was spontaneous-combustion hot. Her mouth went dry, and her face heated into what she knew would be a splendid blush to match her red hair.

"I'll call you back." She dropped the phone in her sweater pocket. "Can I help you?"

"You shouldn't answer the door without checking who it is, especially when you're concerned for your safety." The man's dark brown eyebrows furrowed over his equally dark brown, almost black eyes, and his words hitched her heart into her throat. "You're fortunate I'm from Stryker Security and not someone wanting to hurt you."

June barely refrained from rolling her eyes. She'd been doing that too much lately, though in her defense, it normally was a direct consequence of an obnoxious man. She already regretted buckling to her father's demands, handsome security guard or not.

"It's nice to meet you, too. I'm Reagan MacArthur, by the way."

The elevator dinged, and she glanced down the hall. Her hamburger needed to get here stat. Hangry June itched under the surface, and a cocky, overbearing bodyguard might be the addition to the equation that equaled a full-blown meltdown. She mentally slumped when more Joes got off the elevator, toting duffles and gear like they were preparing to storm Area 51. Thankfully, the loft suite only shared the hall with a few other rooms. She could keep her private secret service ... well, a secret.

She stepped back and motioned for the men to enter. "Please, come in. Make yourselves comfortable. There's a loft up the stairs with two queen beds. You'll have to bunk up or something. One of you can grab the couch."

Tall, dark, and cranky stepped past and stopped next to her, a spicy scent wafting with him and making her stomach growl again. Great. Incredibly handsome *and* smelled good enough to take a bite out of. He glanced at her stomach, his eyebrow raising as he lifted his gaze to meet hers.

"I have food coming," she mumbled as she covered her stomach with her hand.

"I know." His words and slight smirk reminded her of her earlier comment, making her neck and face heat again. "I'm Sosimo Rivas. I'm in charge of your security detail for this weekend."

Wonderful. He had the sexy accent to go with the package. Why couldn't her head of security be some retired colonel with shaggy gray eyebrows and overgrown nose hairs? Being a self-conscious nerd growing up with an overbearing father hadn't afforded a ton of opportunities to practice taming her propensity for blushing around guys. Since she spent most of her adult life in her lab, she hadn't really improved her high school dilemma much. Her geeky, introvert-self dreaded what was sure to be a weekend filled with mortifying moments.

As one good-looking guy after another walked into her suite, she wondered if it was too late to take her chances with whoever had sent those emails. Mr. Rivas introduced his team by throwing names at her faster than her food-deprived brain could grab them. The elevator dinged, and she leaned out in hopes her food had arrived. Mr. Rivas's shoulders, covered by a coat that molded perfectly to his frame, invaded her vision as he stepped in front of her. With a huff, she let the door go and walked into the suite. The sound of the door thumping against Mr. Serious's back was oddly satisfying.

One guy with auburn hair and a thick, trimmed beard whistled long and low. "Nice digs you got here."

"Yeah, since I planned on being here a few weeks, I wanted to have a larger space to spread out in." June crossed her arms, the excess of the room making her feel self-conscious. Even though she had sold her first invention for several billion dollars five years ago, the lavish lifestyle didn't settle right on her.

"I'm Reagan." She held out her hand.

The man gave her an enormous smile as he wrapped his large hand around hers and pumped it. "Rafe. Nice to meet you, Reagan."

She smiled and hoped she looked at ease as the others reintroduced themselves. The door pushed open, and the room service cart rattled into the room. The poor delivery man looked like he'd been water boarded. His eyes were wide and sweat beaded across his forehead.

She rushed over and smiled at him. "Thank you so much."

He nodded and his lips trembled up in more of a grimace than anything else. "You're welcome. My pleasure, ma'am."

June followed him to the door, grabbing her purse on the entry table, and giving him a large tip. Sosimo stood guarding the door, his arms crossed over his massive chest. The hotel worker ducked his head and rushed out the door and down the hall like his life depended on it.

She crossed her arms and glared at Sosimo. "Was that necessary? You just scared ten years off that dear man's life."

"You never know who might pose as a worker just to get to you. Rafe. Leave it." Sosimo's harsh order caused her to jump and turn around.

Rafe peeked under the cover on the tray. He slammed it shut with a chagrined look and a shrug. "It smells good."

These were the guys Dad insisted were the best? "Go ahead, Rafe. I can order something else." June waved toward the tray, her stomach protesting the thought of waiting longer.

"No, you can eat that. Your stomach is making more noise than a Ford power steering pump low on fluid. We'll order more food." Sosimo grabbed her elbow and pulled her toward the dining room table. "Why don't you sit and eat while you tell us what the plan is for this weekend?"

Sosimo pulled the chair out for her and pushed it in as she sat down, dragging the tray close. She would have protested, but the smell from the plate as the lid lifted had her stomach roaring.

"You hiding a tiger somewhere in your shirt?" Rafe's eyes grew wide as he peeked under the table.

June laughed as her face heated. "No, no tiger. I just got so busy I forgot to eat."

"You do that often?" Sosimo's eyebrows scrunched low over his eyes, and she felt as if he criticized her.

She shrugged. "The dilemma of a busy mind, I guess. Order whatever you want. They have great food here."

June lifted her hamburger, the juices dripping out of the burger onto her plate. She couldn't eat this without making a mess, but at this point, she couldn't care less. She didn't want to impress any of these guys anyway, good-looking or not. She took a bite and groaned as the rich flavor hit her tongue. She'd have to remember to eat more often. She closed her eyes and savored the bite. When she opened them, all the men stared at her. She put the hamburger down on the plate and dabbed her mouth with her napkin as she tried to regain any dignity she may have left.

"I think I'll order one of those." Derrick's deep voice rumbled into the quiet room.

Rafe jumped up and rushed to the phone. "I'll call it in."

"Order me one too," Jake called from where he was setting up gear.

"Sos, you want something?" Rafe asked with the phone to his ear.

Sosimo shook his head, still staring at June.

"Your loss, man." Rafe turned his attention to the person on the other end of the phone.

June picked up her burger and attempted to take smaller bites. Eating under Sosimo's scrutiny unnerved her and ruined her enjoyment of the meal. She took two more bites and ate a couple fries before she set it down and wiped her fingers on the napkin.

She cleared her throat. "I'm not sure how much you know about what's going on this weekend, but I have put together a poker tournament to raise money for the A Hero's Tomorrow Foundation. Do you know of that foundation?"

Sosimo's eyebrows rose, and he cast a quick look toward Jake. "We've heard of it."

"I've set the weekend up like the poker tournament in *Maverick*. The winner will split the pot with the foundation. In fact, the movie inspired me."

"*Maverick*? That's cool." Rafe sat down across from her at the table.

She smiled back. "So the tournament will start tonight after dinner ends, and it'll go until the last person wins, which should be sometime tomorrow, at the latest Sunday."

"You should get people coming in just to watch." Derrick placed some gear in front of Rafe.

"I hope so. I've already raised twenty-five million dollars, and that was just in the registration for the poker players. I'm hoping to raise more over the weekend with bystanders and the different silent auctions and whatnot I have set up around the room."

"Well, hopefully your event doesn't end like the one in the movie did ... with theft. Gambling doesn't attract the best of characters." Sosimo crossed his arms where he leaned against the back of the couch.

June grabbed up her hamburger and tore another bite off, imagining it was Sosimo's condescending attitude. She should've known that her dad would have her hire someone just like him. Sosimo better not ruin this weekend for her or she'd be more than hangry—she'd go supernova on the Latin heartthrob.

SOSIMO TUGGED on the sleeve of his tux again as they meandered through the crowd. Reagan had been explicit about wanting the four of them to blend in as much as possible. She'd also only allowed one of them to stay close to her. Sosimo hadn't liked the idea, but she had been firm on that decision. So he stuck to her side and smiled at people as participants and spectators filed into the hotel ballroom.

"Is everything going okay, Mandy?" Reagan asked the brown-haired young woman who approached with a clipboard.

Mandy nodded, tapping her pen on the paper. "We only have a few participants who haven't arrived yet, but they've already told us they wouldn't be here until after dinner."

"Good. In a couple minutes, I'll do the opening welcome and have everyone get seated for dinner." Reagan touched the necklace around her neck. "I also need you to double che—"

"Reagan, darling, how wonderful to see you." An older woman dressed in a sparkling evening gown and more jewelry than she needed came up and air-kissed Reagan's cheeks.

Sosimo hid a smirk as Reagan's body stiffened, and Mandy's eyes rolled. Who was this woman that would cause such a reaction? She may be influential, but he found her rude, interrupting like she had.

"Good evening, Mrs. Fitzgerald. My, what a lovely dress you have on tonight." Reagan stepped back and admired the woman's outfit that appeared far fancier than what anyone else wore.

Mrs. Fitzgerald placed her hand on her collarbone. "This old thing? Oscar made this for me for a gala last year, but I knew it would be perfect for your little event." She turned her sights to Sosimo, and his throat tightened. "And who is this fine young gentleman?"

"Well ... He's ... He's ..." Reagan stammered.

They had planned to tell anyone who asked that he was a childhood friend. Sosimo wondered how long she'd stutter before she remembered the story she had insisted on. Guess she wasn't as on top of things as she made out.

Mandy's eyes went wide before her mouth opened and words rushed out. "This is Reagan's date. Her boyfriend." Mandy turned a horrified expression to Reagan and mouthed, "I'm sorry," before rushing back to man the door.

"Hoo, hoo. Look's like Sos got the lucky draw of the weekend." Rafe's jest came over the earpiece. "How come I never get stuck with the hot women?"

Reagan's panicked eyes pleaded over Mrs. Fitzgerald's shoulder. She put her hands under her chin and mouthed, "Please."

Sosimo inwardly growled but put on a charming smile as he grabbed Mrs. Fitzgerald's hand. "Sosimo Rivas. Nice to meet you, Señora Fitzgerald."

He thickened his accent as he placed a kiss on her wrinkly hand. He stepped over to Reagan, sliding his arm around her small waist. She stiffened beneath his touch. He swallowed the lump that suddenly formed in his throat.

"It's a pleasure to meet you, as well." Mrs. Fitzgerald fanned herself as she looked toward Reagan. "Splendid job, darling. I wholeheartedly approve."

Sosimo glanced down at Reagan to see how she would respond. She just smiled and nodded at the woman. He flexed his fingers on her waist, the soft fabric snagging on his rough fingers. She peeked up into his face, her dark green eyes questioning him.

Mrs. Fitzgerald chuckled. "Well, I best leave you two lovebirds alone. I have to go find Hubert."

Reagan blushed and cleared her throat, looking back at Mrs. Fitzgerald. "Enjoy your weekend."

"Not as much as you will, I'm sure, darling," Mrs. Fitzgerald said loudly over her shoulder as she walked past, causing several others to look their way.

Sosimo cracked a smile at the old woman's antics and turned to Reagan. He almost burst out laughing at the bright red flush that covered from her neck all the way up her forehead. Her embarrassment at the woman's comment couldn't be passed up. She closed her eyes and rubbed her head before peeking up at him. He cocked his eyebrow.

She groaned and leaned toward him. "I am so, so sorry. I have no clue what Mandy was thinking saying that. She will get a firm talking to when all this is over."

He shrugged and laced his fingers through hers, ignoring the tingle that shot up his arm. "It's all right. It gives me the perfect excuse to stick close to you." Sosimo winked at her, and she swallowed.

"Okay. I'm glad you're not upset." She squeezed his hand, and his heart picked up its beat.

"All part of the day's work." He pointed his chin toward the stage. "Aren't you supposed to be making an announcement or something?"

She startled, pulling him through the crowd toward the stage. Her manner was firmly back to its efficient loftiness.

Sosimo berated himself as he scanned the crowd. He needed to remember to not let her pretty face and big doe eyes distract him. This might be a walk-in-the-park event, but one slip-up could cause disaster.

Plus, something about Reagan sat wrong with him. Up in the room, she had been nothing like he imagined someone worth billions to be like. She seemed down-to-earth, laughing at Rafe's idiotic jokes. She had given them details of the weekend in quick, efficient stats, almost militaristic in the way she took them through the events of the weekend and the participants that had signed up so far.

But the minute she'd walked out of her bedroom with her emerald dress clinging to all the right curves and making his heart pound like a jackhammer, she'd transformed into a billion-dollar woman, complete with the attitude to go with her new persona. The dichotomy unnerved him. He didn't like variables in a mission, and Reagan MacArthur proved a sparkling variable.

She threaded her hand through his elbow. As they walked toward the stage, she happily greeted American royalty and several celebrities like they were old school friends, though her hand slightly trembled on his arm. When they got close to the stage, she leaned in, her flowery scent pushing out all the other smells in the room.

"I've reserved this table right up front for us. Why don't you have a seat while I make my announcement?" Reagan formed it as a question, but her tone made it more like a general's command. He didn't think they taught that in inventor's school.

He surveyed the area and shook his head. "I don't like it. You'll be too exposed."

"Mr. Rivas, you don't have to like it. That's what's going to happen. I can't have you up on the stage with me, even if you are supposed to be my enamored boyfriend. There's no reason for you to get all huffy. The table is close enough should you need to fly to my rescue." With that pronouncement, she took her hand from his elbow and marched up to the stage.

A whistle sounded low and long in his earpiece. "Man, Sos. You got yourself a feisty one." Rafe's jovial tone came across the wire. "How is your happily ever after going for you?"

"Rafe, I thought you had something you were supposed to be doing, like, I don't know, maybe keeping surveillance on the video feeds?" Sosimo scanned the area until he saw Rafe and stared him down. "Or have all those video games finally rotted your head?"

"Yeah, but that job's not nearly as fun as the job you apparently have this weekend." Rafe winked at him from across the ballroom before turning to go out the door. "I'm off to do the only actual work around here. Don't have too much fun without me."

Sosimo rolled his eyes and went back to surveying the room. Sure, Reagan's beauty surpassed a Colorado sunset over the Rocky Mountains, especially when they first got there and her ginger hair hung in soft waves down her back. But Reagan was not only rich as all get out, but smart. Women like that didn't give poor immigrant men like him a second glance, especially when that man had barely graduated high school. No, he'd be keeping this weekend purely professional, even though he just landed himself the most gorgeous date he'd ever had.

THREE

The next night, June flopped back onto her bed as exhaustion weighed down her legs and arms like the lead weights Special Ops members used in underwater training. Her dress pinched her skin, and she flinched. Who would've known that running a weekend like this would be so tiring? Fundraising proved worse than any of her stretches hermited in her lab, close to breaking through on an invention. That tired invigorated her. This just drained every ounce of life from her. Could she do this again next year like so many had asked, even with raising over fifty million dollars?

She rolled off the bed ungracefully, standing in the dress that kept her from moving properly, and trudged to the dresser for her pajamas. She couldn't wait to get this uncomfortable torture device off and slide beneath the covers. She tossed her sweats and T-shirt onto the bed and reached back to unzip her dress. She groaned and hung her head. How could she have forgotten that she needed help getting in and out of the ridiculous garment?

She glanced at the closed door that led to the living room. One of the guys must still be up. Her fake boyfriend/annoying appendage had made the poor men take rotations keeping guard at night. An all-night guard seemed like overkill. He'd insisted it was necessary in that no-nonsense way he had operated in all weekend. While he kept her skin tingling all weekend with his guiding touches and was hotter than a Hot Tamale, his well-ordered plans and military tendencies had reminded her enough of her father to efficiently douse the tingles. Mostly.

Maybe she could sleep in the dress, then call Mandy to come help before she ventured out of the bedroom in the morning. Wouldn't that just reinforce the princess persona Sosimo had of her? When he'd called her princess for the first time, she'd almost throat punched him. What did it matter anyway? After tomorrow, she'd probably never see him again. Except she'd hired Stryker Security for her investor meeting she'd been able to arrange on Tuesday. Ugh. Two more days, *then* she'd never have to see him again.

The ribbing of her dress pinched her stomach, and she knew sleeping wouldn't happen in the stupid thing. She'd just march out there, ask whoever kept guard to help her out—literally—and march right back into her room. While she was at it, she'd grab her stash of Hot Tamales for a bedtime snack.

She strode to the door and swung it open with deter-mined force. She froze when Sosimo's head snapped up from the computer set up at the table, his tired eyes full of concern. He'd changed into track pants and his T-shirt stretched tight against the muscles of his chest. He'd mussed his hair like he'd been running his hands through it. Maybe she could sleep in the stupid dress.

"Everything okay?" His thick voice sent tendrils of nerves through her stomach.

"Tamales. Hot Tamales." She cringed and closed her eyes at his smirk. "Never mind."

"Hot Tamales sound pretty good right now." He stood and walked toward the kitchenette.

He rolled his neck, rubbing his shoulder. He had to be as exhausted as she was. Maybe she could convince him to just go to sleep. There had been no trouble all weekend long, and she doubted there would be. She could at least try to get him to see reason.

He dug through the basket of candy she'd set up on the counter as she approached, pulling out a box of the cinnamon candies. "Last one. Wanna share?"

"I probably shouldn't have any to begin with, so sharing will keep me from devouring the entire box."

He chuckled, the sound low and much more tempting than the spicy candies he shook into her hand. What was she thinking? She popped one in her mouth, leaning back against the cold counter, and let the sugary concoction refire her brain cells.

"This weekend seemed to go well." Sosimo rested against the counter kitty-corner to her and much too close.

"Yeah, we should be able to help a lot of soldiers with this money."

"What's your connection to the organization?"

"You didn't find out in your team's super-sleuthing?"

She smiled over at him. "I founded the foundation. Wanted to give injured soldiers the best prosthetics possible so they could go back to life. I've been working for years, trying to improve prosthetic limbs. When I went to find an organization that could provide soldiers with rehab and help them get used to their recent addition, I just didn't find one that did everything I wanted them to do. So I started my own."

Sosimo shook another handful of candy into her palm. "Why are you so gung-ho to support the military?"

"Other than the fact the military pays for our freedom in blood and sacrifice every single day?" Her words stilled Sosimo's chewing. She shrugged, hoping to tone down her enthusiasm. "Army brat." She fiddled with the candy. "I guess I saw far too many outstanding men and women not have the support they needed both on the field and off. I want to help however I can." She tossed the candies in her mouth to keep herself from revealing more.

"You're helping. More than you'll ever know." Sosimo twisted the box of candy in his hands. "Your invention? We call it Superman how it allows us to see things through walls."

She smiled. "I like that name. Too bad it's trademarked."

"Anyway, it saved our entire unit on more than a few missions. Wish it could be available for every mission."

"It's not?" Her heart dropped. She had ramped up production to make sure the military had plenty available.

Sosimo shook his head. "Would've saved our friend

Ethan Stryker's life and Jake's leg if we'd had that on our last mission together."

"Jake?" She touched her neck as she looked up the stairs, tears stinging her eyes.

"Yeah. His right leg has one of your fancy prosthetics. He has a few of them, actually."

"I'm sorry about your friend and about Jake." She shook her head. "I don't understand. I provided the military with a lot of those units, much more than they said they needed. Why wouldn't they be available?" She'd have to talk to her father about that.

"Bureaucracy."

"And that's why I started A Hero's Tomorrow and work so closely with the Soldier Enhancement Program. Our soldiers shouldn't have politics get in the way of keeping themselves and us safe." She held her elbow with her hand and ran her other fingers up and down her forehead to alleviate the headache budding between her eyes.

"Reagan." Sosimo placed the candy on the counter and touched her elbow, making her head buzz like she'd eaten two boxes of Hot Tamales. He dropped his hand. "You're tired. Why don't you go to bed?"

"My stupid dress." Her voice only functioned at barely a whisper. "I can't get it off."

The color of his eyes deepened before he cleared his throat and turned his head to look out the windows, though the curtains were drawn. She had been proud of her lack of embarrassment over the weekend, but now her cheeks were hotter than the Sahara Desert and probably as red as a beet. Curse her father's Irish genetics that showed her slightest awkwardness or tinge of anger.

"I'm sorry. I'd call Mandy, but I don't want to wake her up." She fiddled with the front of the dress. "I'd just sleep in it, but the dumb thing pokes me in the ribs every time I move."

"It's no problem." He turned back to her, his face a blank mask. "I have sisters. I know how it goes. Turn." He swirled his index finger in a circle, all officer-in-command again.

She turned and gulped as he pushed her hair over her shoulders and deftly worked the buttons down her back. "If you just go about halfway, I can get the rest."

He huffed, the scorching air hitting her skin and sending shivers down her exposed shoulders. "There. Now hit the sack."

"Thanks." She mumbled as she stepped away from him. She half-turned, keeping her gaze on the floor. "Good night."

She rushed to her room as fast as the tight dress and her remaining dignity allowed. Whoever designed dresses to bind thighs together so a woman couldn't stride was an idiot. This dress would burn the first chance she got.

When she reached the door, Sosimo's soft words teased her ear. "Good night, princess."

She closed the door with more force than necessary and leaned against it. Her reaction to the arrogant man angered her. He may attract her. May make her feel hotter than an armadillo in the Texas desert in summer when she neared him. That just meant she spent way too much time alone in her lab rather than socializing in the real world.

After this weekend finished and she proposed her latest invention to the Soldier Enhancement Program, she needed to get serious about dating, maybe even sign up for one of those dating sites. Her thirty-one-year-old ovaries were working overtime if she found herself attracted to the exact type of man she always avoided like the plague.

She thought of Landon, her ex, who'd stolen her heart and then tried to steal her Superman invention. Well, she didn't always avoid military men, which explained why she needed to keep her reactions to Señor Hotstuff under control. She got ready for bed as quick as she could, listing all the reasons why she didn't like Sosimo in her head until she fell asleep.

TWO DAYS LATER, if Sosimo could roll his shoulders without drawing attention to himself, he would. The meeting with Reagan's potential investors had lasted long —hours longer than they had expected. While Reagan's invention impressed him, his gut told him something wasn't right. He had tried to push down the anxiety, had prayed for God to calm him, but the tango his nerves were dancing only increased, and he would not take the warning lightly.

As everyone shuffled to leave, he approached Reagan, whispering his concern into the com. Man, she looked beautiful with her face all glowing in pride. He wanted to be wrong and that the people here actually had an interest in her invention. From what he'd gathered over the weekend, even if they weren't, she'd fund the project herself, not caring how much it cost her.

He stepped close, kissed her cheek to keep up the doting boyfriend act, and whispered in her ear. "Good job. Now we get you out of here."

She pulled back, her face an inch from his. Her eyebrows furrowed before a false smile stretched across her lips. "Thanks, honey. I'll walk these ladies and gentlemen to the lobby, then we can head out." She turned to the group. "Thank you again for coming. I hope that you are enjoying Aspen while you're here. If there are no other questions, Mr. Rivas reminded me I have an important phone call I'm to make. Sorry I kept you here so long. I get very excited about this opportunity for helping our armed forces, and I forget about everything else."

She laughed, the sound insincere to his ears. The others laughed with her, nodding their heads and commenting on being accused of doing the same. The entire situation reeked of false fronts and lies and had his skin crawling.

Reagan sauntered toward the door, leaving Sosimo to catch up. He lengthened his stride, then threaded his fingers through hers. Her hand felt clammy and trembled. How much of what she did was a facade? Zeke stepped up next to her other side, and Sosimo breathed easier, glad they'd pulled Zeke in for this meeting.

"Miss MacArthur, I find your invention fascinating. I thought gear like that was only available in the movies." Zeke smiled that smile that made women of all ages swoon.

Sosimo wanted to punch the look right off him. He shook his head and scanned the walkway to the lobby. What was wrong with him? Zeke had no interest in Reagan. Samantha and Eva had fully sieged his heart. Sosimo's reaction stunk of jealousy, and he didn't like it. Who cared if he couldn't stop thinking of her flowery scent or how hard she'd pushed herself over the weekend to benefit soldiers? He had to focus, get this job done, and get Miss Fancy Pants on her way. Then he'd find a project car to fix, and life would get back to normal.

"Rafe, are we good?" Sosimo spoke low to distract himself.

"We're ready. I positioned the undercover cops in the lobby with Derrick and Jake. I'm packing everything up now." Rafe rustled something with a grunt. "We'll be ready to drop the package off at the airport as soon as she's done jaw jacking and packs her stuff from her room."

Sosimo had suggested involving the local police though they normally didn't, but with the way his nerves were firing at high alert, he was glad he had made the call. He tightened his hold on Reagan's hand, inhaling slowly through his nose while he scanned the lobby.

She glanced down at their hands, then up at him, her bottom lip drawing in between her teeth. "Sosimo is everythi—"

A vase exploded into shards of glass, flowers flying wildly as Zeke hollered, "Contact, front."

Sosimo turned, pushing Reagan sideways. A force slammed into his bulletproof vest, knocking the breath out of him and throwing him forward. Crap. He wrapped

Reagan in his arms as he fell. When they hit the ground, he covered her with his body, praying she'd be safe. She whimpered, her body shaking in violent tremors.

"Shh, it's okay," he choked out over the pain radiating across his back. "I've got you."

She clung to his shirt, burying her face in his neck. He could hear her hurried prayers over the rapid firing that surrounded them. Then as quickly as it began, the shooting stopped. Shouts filled the air, and screams echoed through the lobby.

"Clear?" Sosimo lifted his head a few inches to survey the damage.

"Clear." Zeke's voice sounded strained.

Sosimo pried Reagan's fingers from his shirt and pushed back onto his knees with a groan. She scrambled up next to him, her face streaked with tears and hair half falling from its updo. Her gaze swiveled to take in the lobby, landing on him with wide eyes. Her mouth flapped open and closed, and tears filled her eyes.

He lifted his hand, ignoring the pain that shot across his shoulders, and brushed the hair from her face. "It's over now. You're okay." He rubbed her cheek with his thumb. "Looks like you needed us after all."

A sob shuddered out of her, and he pulled her close. This job had just taken a turn for the worse.

"Sos, we're leaving." Zeke reached out his hand and pulled Reagan up.

Sosimo shook off the feeling of emptiness.

Reagan gasped. "You're hit." She gingerly reached towards Zeke's sleeve saturated in crimson blood.

"It's just a scratch." Zeke waved her off as he reached

the uninjured hand to pull Sosimo up. "I saw you take that hit. You okay?" The concern in his eyes belied the sharp tone of voice.

"It'll bruise, but I'm fine." Sosimo reached for Reagan and pulled her to his side. "Let's get to the vehicle."

Zeke nodded. "The cops said they'd clean things up and get with us later."

Sosimo scanned the hotel one last time. Five men lay dead in different positions. One of them had sat next to him during the meeting. The hairs on the back of his neck rose. He wanted out of here stat.

Jake took point as Zeke and Derrick surrounded him and Reagan. They rushed through the hotel, emerging from a side door to Rafe waiting with the vehicle. He pushed Reagan in, then got in behind her.

She turned to him as the others circled the SUV and loaded up. "You're shot?"

"I'm fine. Vest took the impact." He hoped to comfort her, but the way her eyes widened and she bit her lip, he didn't think he'd succeeded. "Buckle up."

She nodded, pulling the seatbelt over her shoulder. Her hands shook with such force that she couldn't fit the buckle into the connector. With a gentle touch, he took it from her hands and buckled her in. He moved his hand away, but she grabbed it before he could. She threaded her fingers through his and clung tightly with both hands. As she laid her head on his shoulder with a sigh, Sosimo flexed his fingers in hers and stared out the window at the stars in the black sky. It didn't look like he would get rid of the princess any time soon.

FOUR

June tossed the hairbrush down on the bed. Her hands shook, so she crossed her arms and tucked them close to her. Two days should've been enough time to get over the shock of being in a shootout, but her hands didn't agree.

Maybe the shakes were because of her lack of sleep rather than the actual gun fight. She couldn't help it. Every night when she lay her head down and finally drifted off, she would jerk awake from the recurring nightmare that haunted her nights. She'd wake up gasping, the weight of Sosimo, as he protected her in her dream, so real it bound her chest like it had in Aspen. Only, in her dream the hot stickiness of blood would seep through the back of her shirt. She always awoke when she rolled him off her, his eyes glazed over in death from the hole in his chest. She hated that dream.

She huffed, shook her hands out, and stomped out of the room. Maybe today they could figure out a plan for getting her invention to the right people. If she got away from Sosimo and this platoon of testosterone, maybe the dreams would stop plaguing her.

Her phone blared the trumpet call *Reveille,* and she groaned. "Good morning, Dad."

"Good morning? A good morning would include waking up and enjoying a hot cup of coffee while reading the morning news." Her father's voice sounded extra cranky this morning. "Imagine my surprise when I find an article about my daughter being in the middle of a shootout with terrorists."

"That was in today's paper? It happened two days ago."

"I was catching up on the news, and don't change the subject. Why didn't you call?"

"Honestly? It happened so late, and then yesterday was so packed with cleaning up the mess that I just forgot." She rubbed her forehead, guilt thickening her throat. "I haven't really been myself. I'm sorry. I should've called."

Her father sighed deeply on the other end. "I know how it is after a battle. Are you okay? You weren't hurt?"

She continued down the stairs. "I'm fine. The men you had me hire had the situation under control before I even had time to think."

"Good. They're good men."

"I'm here at their complex until we figure things out. I'm staying under their protection until there's no longer a threat."

He sighed deeply again. "Thank you, Junebug. Thank you for doing that."

"Dad, I promise. I'll be safe. These guys are G.I. Joe on steroids."

"They better be. The Army Special Operations doesn't produce flakes." Her dad's voice got the Army-proud tone to it.

"I gotta go, Dad. I love you."

"Love you too, Junebug."

She tucked her phone into her pocket as she walked into the kitchen. The tightness in her chest for forgetting to call him had eased. She'd have to remember to call her mom later to relieve her worry. Though knowing her mom, she had fretted little. Her parents were such contrasts it amazed her that their marriage had worked. Where her dad proved all rough and controlling, her mom was laid back and gentle. She often said there was no point in worrying when she could just take it to God and let Him handle it. Maybe their differences made their relationship work?

She just needed to find a guy that was her complete opposite, then she'd have the workings of a great relationship. But which her? She paused as she reached for the coffeepot. June, the introverted nerd who could spend hours and days tinkering with an invention with no social contact, had always been her go-to girl. But since the need for Reagan became more necessary as the foundation and her company expanded, the outgoing people-person grew on her.

She shook her head and grabbed the coffee. Was she just arguing over which version of herself she really was? Not good, not good at all. Thankfully, Samantha and her adorable daughter, Eva, rushed into the house at that point and distracted her from her confusing inner struggle.

"Good morning." June's voice trailed off at the look on Sam's face. "What's wrong?"

"I don't know." Sam held tight to Eva as she glanced out the door. "Something's wrong with Tina, but Zeke wouldn't tell me."

"Who's Tina?" June asked as the sound of a vehicle slamming its brakes in the rocks screeched outside.

"The nanny." Sam's breathless voice caused goose-bumps to breakout across June's skin.

She clutched the coffee mug tightly in her hand and stared out the front door like Sam. Anticipation built in her chest like a wet, heavy blanket. Sosimo stomped through the door, his presence lifting the stifling feeling. One look at his expression slammed it back over her.

"Come, now." He grabbed Eva from Sam's arms and without another word led them through the house to the basement.

He clicked a code into a keypad beside a door, which whooshed open with a groan. The thick door must weigh a ton. June's dread weighted her feet so she had difficulty moving. Sosimo glared at her as he pushed the door closed.

He put Eva down and pointed to a basket full of books in the corner. "Why don't you go pick out a book to look through?"

She rushed off to the basket, and Sosimo turned to a computer mounted to the wall. With two clicks, he had surveillance feeds up on the wall of screens. One screen showed the guys searching a car. A cute young woman sat crying in the driver's seat.

"Sos, what's going on?" Sam voiced the question of the day.

He glanced at June before turning back to the screen. "Reagan's admirers strapped a bomb to Tina's car."

June's heart dropped to her toes and blood pounded in her ears. Everything faded to the movement on the screen. Her breath stuttered out when the woman jumped from the car, only to suck back in as Zeke reached into the car.

Sosimo pointed to another screen as the car careened across the backyard. The boom and shake of the floor twisted June's gut. Feeling rushed back to her hands and feet, almost buckling her knees.

Eva whimpered, pulling June's gaze to her precious face. June had to leave this place, go somewhere away from these innocent people. Maybe Reagan should disappear forever, and June could quietly take control of her life again. Because under Reagan's management, she'd almost just gotten the nanny blown up.

SOSIMO'S GUT twisted with the weight of what needed to be done. The lack of color in Reagan's face had made him wish he had time to pull her into his arms and let her know it would all be okay. His anger toward the men who did this made his brain threaten to flush with the need of violence. He took a deep breath to cleanse the emotion away and rushed up the stairs to the living room.

He marched to the fireplace and got right to business. "I'm taking her, just the two of us. I just put in a call to Cooper Ford. Remember, he just retired? He's going to meet us in Amarillo. We'll stay low as we travel to Fort Belvoir for her meeting." He rubbed his neck as he paced. "If you guys are up for a bait and switch, you all could pretend to take her from here with flair, maybe get the jet and fly, changing flight plans before you land. If I take the Cinnamon from the old garage, she can lie in the backseat until we are away from here. Have some Mexican music blaring and my hat pulled low, and anyone left watching the complex hopefully won't connect me to here."

Derrick nodded. "I'll go get a pack together from the stables. You'll want body armor and weapons."

"I'll help." Jake stood, and the two rushed out the front door.

"Excuse me." Tina stood from the stool at the kitchen island. "I'd like to help. I could pretend to be whoever it is you're protecting. Make it more believable."

Sosimo was amazed by her bravery. "It's not safe, Tina. Whoever is after her could attack."

She smirked and shrugged. "I'd love to get back at them for blowing up Sweetpea. That car still had lots of miles left to her."

"Okay, you'll have to wrap your head, maybe wear sunglasses, but I think it will work."

Reagan came up the stairs. Her lips still lacked color and the freckles splashed across her nose seemed extra bright on her skin. She didn't deserve this, not when all she wanted was to help keep soldiers safe. His jaw clenched in frustration.

"Reagan." His sharp tone snapped her head to him. He tried to soften his voice. "Pack your gear. We leave in ten."

From the way she flinched and stumbled up the stairs to the bedroom, he didn't think he'd succeeded in the entire softening affair. He shrugged it off and turned to Rafe. He didn't have time to coddle her anyway.

"You'll need communication that can't be tracked. New IDs for her." Rafe tugged on his beard. "I'll get on that and get a laptop set up for you."

Sosimo clapped him on the shoulder. "Thanks."

Rafe smiled, that gleam in his eye that always made Sosimo partly dread and partly anticipate what would spew out of the goofball's mouth. "You know what they say about road trips?" Rafe cocked his eyebrow. "They're the perfect opportunity for love to drive right into your heart."

Sosimo rolled his eyes at the ludicrous thought.

"Seriously, Sos. Think about all that time alone ... just the two of you." Rafe rounded the corner of the couch as he headed to the tech room. "It's the perfect recipe for love."

"Just stop." Sosimo chucked Eva's stuffed animal at Rafe. "We'll only be alone for a day."

Rafe laughed and headed downstairs, singing loudly, "And I would walk five-hundred miles ..."

Sosimo shook his head as he walked to the hallway and placed his finger on the print lock for the drawers. Where did Rafe come up with this stuff? Sosimo thought about the way Reagan smelled like a field of flowers and how soft her hair had been when he'd moved it aside to unbutton her dress. He froze as the drawer clicked open, his fingers aching with the wonder of what it would feel like to take his time with the long soft tresses.

Dang, Rafe. Sosimo cleared his throat and forced himself to focus on the task at hand. He couldn't afford to get distracted. He couldn't screw up another person's life. He grabbed his holster and handgun he kept stored in the drawer and put it on. He glanced at his watch and rushed up the stairs to push Reagan into hurrying.

Her door was open, so he strode in. One of the bags he and Derrick had brought back from the hotel the day before sat on the bed with clothes half shoved in. His hand paused as he reached to push the clothes the rest of the way into the bag. Had they watched the hotel suite? Did he and Derrick lead these men to the ranch by not being more careful when they went to Aspen to tie up the loose strings? Ice raced down his spine as sounds of weeping filtered from the attached bathroom.

He moved to the open door, his heart slowing and his throat aching. Reagan kneeled, curled over the toilet, her hair a curtain covering her face. When the retching stopped, great sobs shook her body. He grabbed a wash-cloth from the sink, ran cold water over it, and brought it to her.

"Reagan?" He touched her shoulder only to have her curl away, laying her head on her arm draped across the toilet seat.

Kneeling beside her, he ran his hand across her back. "It'll be okay."

She shook her head. He placed the washcloth in her

hand. Her fingers clenched tightly around it before she brought it to her forehead.

"I almost got that woman killed." Hiccups interrupted her voice.

"No, that's not your fault."

She sat up quickly. Crying had turned her eyes red and her skin blotchy. Hair sprung wildly about her face, making her look like a wrung-out fairy.

"How can you say that?" Her eyelids bunched closed, and she pulled at the hair beside her temples. "What if Eva had been hurt?"

She leaned over the toilet and heaved again. Sosimo's ribs tightened around his chest, making it hard for him to fill his lungs. He pulled her hair out of the way, holding it until she finished. Gently, he pried the washcloth out of her hand, flushed, and eased her head off the seat.

He cleared his throat as he wiped her face. "This isn't your fault."

"It is. And you hate me for it." She turned to look at the wall.

"I don't hate you." His skin tingled with her words. "Why would you say that?"

"I saw it in your eyes. You practically blazed a hole through me with your glare." She pulled her knees to her chest and shuddered out a whimper as she laid her head on her knees. "I don't blame you. I'm not too fond of myself either right now."

His stomach turned that he made her feel such guilt. He was a class-act jerk. He moved closer, leaning his head on hers.

"I don't hate you." His voice barely passed the tightness in his throat.

She looked up, a crease in her forehead as her green eyes gazed at him. "You don't?"

He shook his head and rubbed her shoulders. "I was upset with the situation. I'm sorry that I made you think that."

Her shoulders shook with suppressed tears. "I'm scared."

"I know." He barely refrained from telling her he felt the same. "I'll keep you safe. Promise."

Her face crumpled, and he pulled her to him. She twisted her hands into the front of his shirt as sobs shook her slight frame. He wrapped her tighter in his embrace, vowing to himself that he'd fulfill his promise no matter what it cost.

FIVE

Sosimo had pulled out of the hidden garage on the back side of the property half an hour after he left Reagan to finish packing. He'd changed into a button-up western shirt typical of the area and borrowed Derrick's cowboy hat. As the beat-up, 1977 Ford crew cab he'd fixed up a few months ago had rattled and sputtered down the dirt road, he'd questioned if this plan would work.

They had their gear thrown under the camper shell, and Reagan slept on the backseat. He peeked back at her, making sure the blanket stayed pulled up on her shoulders. She'd fallen asleep within the first five minutes of driving past the ranch's main gate and hadn't woken up, even when he stopped to get gas along the way. He understood the exhaustion that hit after an intense adrenaline spike. He hoped she'd sleep for a good while. Though with her already pushing close to three hours, she'd probably be waking soon.

He turned his attention back to the road, thinking about how she'd surprised him. Not only her depth of guilt, but also her ability to push past that emotion so they could get on the road quickly. She'd only cried for a couple of minutes, pulling herself together and getting a laser focus on what she needed to take with her. The shift had left him rattled, longing for a few more moments of holding her close.

He slowed as the highway curved around a sharp turn, the mountain walls reaching high into the sky and darkening the road. He'd taken the highway south, heading over the mountain and down toward New Mexico. He wanted to avoid the interstate and major cities as much as possible, especially at first. Maybe then, whoever wanted to get Reagan would lose her trail long enough for them to make it to Virginia.

Something about all of this left his mind tangled and bunched, like words on the page often became from his dyslexia. He should be able to understand what was going on, but he couldn't make sense of it. The emails she'd gotten had sounded like they wanted control of the invention, but then strapping a bomb to Tina's car and demanding Reagan, made it seem like they wanted her. Why did they come out with guns blazing at the hotel? It made little sense. If he wouldn't have jumped in front of her and taken a bullet to the back, she'd probably be dead.

He'd told Rafe to dig and dig deep. The way these guys operated left Sosimo cold and clammy.

Sosimo pulled into Ouray, Colorado, craning his neck at how the mountains opened up to nestle the town deep in the valley. The gorgeous landscape reminded him of the leave he'd taken in Switzerland. This might be a place he'd like to come to after all this blew over. He found a spot to park on the main street. He needed to stretch his legs before getting back on the road. He put the truck in park and turned off the ignition.

Reagan sat up and gazed out the windows. The glassy eyes and fabric crease along her cheek showed a vulnerability that dropped boulders in his gut.

"Where are we?" She peered out the opposite window.

"Ouray, Colorado."

"It's beautiful. I feel like I'm in the Alps." She brushed her hair with her fingers.

"My thoughts exactly." He put his arm on the back of the seat so he could look at her. "We'll find someplace to eat lunch before heading on."

"Great. I'm starving." Her stomach stressed her statement with a growl.

Sosimo chuckled as he got out and peered around. This place had an amazing small town vibe with the old houses that appeared to have been there for decades and the one street that drove the short length from one side to the other. The townspeople had built most of the buildings on Main Street in the style of architecture of the budding Old West—impressive stone buildings and false fronts. Any minute a horse could meander down the extra wide road and no one would take a second look. He could see to the opposite end of town where the highway curved up the side of the mountain heading farther south. With the walls of the mountains jutting up close on all sides, Ouray had nowhere to grow and expand.

As he waited for Reagan to get out of the truck,

Sosimo took a minute to scan the people for trouble. He could definitely tell who the tourists were with their stocking hats, puffy North Face jackets, and completely put-together faces. That brand of upscale outdoorsy people so prevalent in Colorado. He also knew who the locals were by the no-nonsense looks on their faces and the cowboy cut of their jeans.

The door to the truck screeched open, and Reagan stepped out. Her ginger hair peeked out of his ball cap, flowing down her back. She'd pulled a vest over her plaid shirt. Something about her casual look and the fact that she wore his hat hit him like a freight train. His mouth went dry at how unassuming and beautiful she was. While she'd never blend in anywhere with her stunning looks, she appeared like she'd just pulled in from down the street.

"I hope you don't mind." She pointed to the army green hat with the American flag on it. "I couldn't find anything to tame my hair with."

He swallowed and shook his head. "Nope. Glad you found something. Hope it's not too nasty."

She smiled and shoved her hands in her vest pockets. "Not too gross. Not nearly as bad as how I get sometimes when I'm working on an invention." She started walking down the street, and he fell in beside her.

"Really?"

"Once, I had stayed in the same outfit for six days." She chuckled. "When I finally crawled my way out of my lab, my hair was a greasy mess and I reeked of stale coffee and B.O."

He smiled at the thought of her like that. "I'm sure

it's nothing compared to how I smelled after some missions I had to go on. This one time we hitched a ride into a hot zone in a truck full of goats."

"No." Her eyes sparkled up at him.

He nodded. "It was a four-hour ride in. The temp reached into the hundreds about a quarter of the way there. I've never smelled anything as pungent as hot goats in a contained area. I ended up washing my gear three times before I got the smell out."

"Okay, yeah. You've got me beat." She turned in a circle, an awestruck look upon her face. "I love it here. I wish we had time to explore."

"Me too." Sosimo pointed to a waterfall that snaked a thin trail down the mountain. "Maybe after things settle down." His brain skidded to a halt as she gazed up at him and bit her lip. "That is, maybe you can come after things settle."

Her face fell slightly before she pasted on a smile and nodded. "I'll have to look into it."

He pointed to the Red Mountain Brewery. "How does that sound?"

"As long as they have a big juicy burger and crispy fries, I'm in."

Sosimo pulled the door open for her and motioned her in. The smell of fried food and cheerful talking assaulted his senses, waking him up to his idiocy. He couldn't forget that this was a job, and she was a client. Besides, no matter how down-to-earth or beautiful she was now, she was part of the tangle that kept his mind spinning. There were too many sides to Reagan MacArthur that made little sense, too many inconsistencies that whispered she wasn't divulging all the truth. Liars always left him with a gritty feeling that rubbed him raw. Falling for one would inevitably pour salt in the wound.

JUNE STARED out the window at the passing scenery and bemoaned the fact that they had left the Rocky Mountains behind for the New Mexican desert. She could happily stay in the mountains forever. Maybe because it reminded her of when her father had been stationed in Germany and her brother was still alive. As a family, they'd traveled the mountains and small European villages almost every time her father didn't have to work. Even though they hadn't been there long, it held some of her happiest memories.

She peeked over at Sosimo where he strummed his fingers to the pop rock music playing on the radio. Maybe her desire to retreat to the rocky peaks and deep valleys had more to do with the vibrant man beside her than the ghosts of happiness from her past. The churning of her stomach and the tightening of her chest eased when he neared. She shouldn't layer emotion onto simple words, but when he'd said he didn't hate her, that his anger was for the men and not her, all the tension had drained out of her into the fancy bathroom tiles, seeping through the grout.

She looked back out the window at the monotonous tan landscape flashing by. Just because he didn't hate her, didn't mean he felt anything else beyond a sense of duty.

He'd barely said more than ten words since they'd eaten lunch in Ouray. The lack of communication wasn't awkward, just silent.

She was just a part of his job, and she needed to remember that.

Convincing her brain to stop replaying the image of him reading a story to Eva to calm her after the bomb, or the feel of his arms tight around her as she bawled her eyes out, was next to impossible though. And she needed to stop inhaling the spicy scent filling every inch of the cab that somehow made her nerves relax and her heart rate increase at the same time. The mixed signals her body kept reporting to her brain just might short-circuit it, leaving her an incompetent fool.

Geesh. It wasn't like him holding her had been romantic in any way. Talk about an embarrassing moment. She cringed. Why did he have to catch her tossing her cookies? If only her emotions weren't so tied to her gut. Oh, to handle emotional situations without the bubbly feeling threatening to erupt. Since she'd been that way through the upheavals of her childhood, it probably wouldn't be changing soon.

She grabbed the bag of Swedish Fish she'd bought at the last gas stop and popped one in her mouth. She'd have to remember to get more snacks next time they gassed up. Sosimo must be a robot or something, not requiring food on a regular basis to operate. She remained more a feast or famine type of person. When her brain ran nonstop, simple things like eating went out the window. Any other time, she'd fit in well with the hobbits.

"Why don't you search for a low-key place to stay?" Sosimo's voice startled her as he pointed at the billboard on the side of the road. "We're almost to Tucumcari."

"Okay." She pulled up lodgings on her phone. "Low-key?" She slid her finger along the screen, scanning through the options.

"Not someplace with many people. See if you can find an older motel or something."

She smiled when a picture of the Blue Swallow Motel came up. It was charming in a *Cars* cartoon sort of way. Though with her luck, it'd probably end up more like *Psycho*. She ignored the shiver that raced up her body and called the motel.

"All right. We have a room at the Blue Swallow."

Sosimo scowled, and his hands tightened on the steering wheel.

The Swedish Fish twisted and flopped in her belly, like it always did when she disappointed people. "You want me to find a different place?"

Too bad the money she made from that first invention couldn't have bought her some confidence when it came to dealing with people. In some situations she could fake it, especially when in a crowd or if it involved her inventions. One-on-one revealed a different story, making her doubt every word and action.

She blamed it on the constant moving as a child that had drained her, causing her to spend all her time buried in books and tinkering instead of making new friends. What was the point when she'd have to make fresh ones in a few years anyway? In hindsight, that probably wasn't the best mode of operation since the only person she now considered a friend was her assistant Mandy. Could she even count someone as a friend when she paid them?

"That should work. I don't like the sound the truck is making." He checked the rearview mirror. "It's been whining at me since we left the ranch."

"Your truck talks to you?" She wondered at the tinge of pink that rose up the back of his neck and leaned her back against the door to observe him better.

"Don't your inventions speak to you, tell you when something isn't right?" He turned his attention to her, his deep brown eyes boring straight to her soul.

A tingling sensation hit her nose. She gulped and nodded. No one had ever understood that about her.

He shrugged and turned his attention back to the road. "It's the same with me and motors. They tell me what's wrong, and I fix them. They are just about the only thing I can understand." His cheek muscle jumped as he clenched his teeth and cleared his throat.

"Well, it looks like we have something in common. Not sure if having inanimate objects speaking to us is necessarily a good trait to share. Most just find that weird." She gripped her phone and groaned. "Not that I find you weird or anything. I'm the weird one—me and my enormous mouth. Are you hungry? I'm starving. It looks like there are a couple of places within walking distance of the motel."

She swiped her finger on the screen, wishing she could escape. Being stuck in a truck with little more than two feet separating her from the sexiest man alive—yes, *People* magazine got it wrong—was detrimental to her language processing system. Not that she'd had much of a system to begin with.

He stopped at a streetlight and looked at her. His eyes shone as he gazed at her, a slow smile building on his face. The air became thick. She licked her parched lips, and his gaze darted to them.

"Oh sí, tengo hambre." His accent came out thick. "Very hungry."

He swallowed as the light changed green and turned east onto Route 66. Just what kind of kicks did this route have in store for her? They sped up and a loud growling noise startled her out of her silliness. She peered through the back window as if she could see the problem.

"Ay, caray." Sosimo's grip tightened on the steering wheel. "Where's this motel?"

"Less than half a mile up on the left." June scanned the street for the sign. "There."

They pulled into the motel just as a loud pop sounded. Sosimo muttered under his breath as he turned sharply into an empty parking spot and braked. He sat back with a huff and pushed his fingers through his hair.

"I think the rear end just blew." He pulled on his hair before shoving the door open. His frustration ebbed off him in waves.

He slammed the door, and she jumped. She yanked her vest on as she climbed out of the truck. When she got to the rear of the bed, he knelt beside the tire with his head under the truck.

She crouched next to him and peered at the under-carriage, not sure what she looked at. "Well?"

"We're leaking fluid on the differential." His words were as foreign as his Spanish.

"Can you fix it?"

"No. Not here." He brushed his hands together to get the dirt off and stood with a huff. "Let's get checked in and find someplace to eat. There's not much we can do about it tonight."

She nodded and followed him to the motel office. She only blushed a little when he signed them in as John and Sue Hernandez. She pushed the fuzzy feeling aside that seeing her newest fake I.D. connected to his had caused, and enjoyed the charismatic motel.

The place held a nostalgic charm that had her smiling as she surveyed the surrounding businesses. The sun sat low on the horizon and the neon signs blinked on. Her step lightened as they crossed to the cute little salmon-colored building. What a splendid place to break down.

SIX

Of all the places to break down, this had to be one of the worst. Sosimo pushed open the bright blue door to the room and cringed. The hotel had squeezed the two beds into the stamp-sized room. At least there were two beds.

Reagan gasped. "How quaint."

She smiled as she pushed past him into the room. That was one way to put it. He tossed his bag onto the bed closest to the door before she could and rolled his shoulders. She practically climbed over the second bed to peek into the bathroom. His tight chest released its tension at her excitement.

She chuckled as she set her stuff on the other bed. "I love it. Makes me feel like I stepped back in time."

"Let me go grab the rest of our gear and then we'll scrounge up some grub." He closed the door before she could reply and stomped to the truck.

He should've known better than to take the ancient thing, but the cinnamon brown and tan pickup reminded him of his youth fixing vehicles with his uncle. He'd hoped it would keep them under cover, but it turned into a big pain in his butt. He pulled out his phone to check in with Zeke, calling him on the secure line.

"Sos, how'd it go?" Zeke's lack of greeting and tone fit Sosimo's sullen mood perfectly.

"Fine. We made it to Tucumcari, New Mexico."

"Good."

"The truck blew a bearing. I'll have to find some other transportation."

"Your cards don't have limits and can't be traced back to you, Reagan, or the company, so get what you need."

Sosimo nodded even though Zeke couldn't see him. "Is everyone all right there?"

"We haven't had any more threats, and the false trail went perfectly."

"Let's hope they just gave up." Sosimo grabbed the last of the bags from the back of the truck and headed toward the room.

"Wishful thinking." Zeke huffed, a tapping noise coming over the phone, which meant he clicked his pen in frustration.

"Anything else going on?" The tightness in Sosimo's chest had returned.

"Samantha left." His friend's sadness leached through the phone and settled in Sos's gut.

"Ah, man. I'm sorry."

"I don't blame her, not really." Zeke cleared his throat. "Cars blowing up in the yard is a big catalyst to breaking up."

Sosimo didn't know what to say. His own heart broke at never seeing Eva, his little bubble of happiness, again.

He couldn't imagine the anguish that Zeke must be going through.

"Maybe you can go talk to her, let her know that doesn't happen often?" He grabbed at straws.

"Not sure if that would help."

"Might be worth a try."

"Maybe." Zeke's voice trailed off. "Listen. Good job at getting Reagan out of here. Rafe has been digging all day, hasn't come out of his cave downstairs. This problem she has runs deep. Much deeper than we first imagined. He's having trouble untangling all the roots, but as soon as we find something, we'll let you know."

"Great. Thanks for the update."

"He also set up blocks on her phone to bounce the location around, but he says it's not fail-proof."

"I'll just take hers from her, keep it simple."

"Taking a phone from a woman could be dangerous." Zeke chuckled, then sobered. "Keep low, Sos. My gut's not liking this one."

"Copy that. I'll let you know when we get back on the road."

Sosimo ended the call and pushed open the hotel room door.

"I'll keep you posted." Reagan had her phone smashed between her shoulder and her ear as she braided her hair. "Bye."

She leaned over the bed, letting the phone drop to the comforter. She twisted a rubber band around her thick braid, her smile fading as she glanced at him.

"Everything okay?" Her forehead got that crease it did when something concerned her.

"Who was that?" His voice came out gruffer than necessary. Maybe he needed to find some food before he opened his mouth again.

"Adam." She cleared her throat. "Colonel Adam Johnson. He's my contact at the SEP. I was letting him know we are on the way."

"No contacting anyone from here on out. Not until we get some answers." He dumped the bags on the floor and dug through them, pulling out a burner phone. "In fact, we need to keep your phone off so they can't trace it."

He crossed the few steps it took to get to her phone, dropped the extra one down, and picked up hers.

"What? Wait! I've known Adam my whole life. He's one of my father's best friends."

Why did he feel such relief that Adam was her father's age? It shouldn't matter to him. It did, though, a lot.

"Doesn't matter. Until we figure out how they tracked you to the ranch, we go dark, only contacting the team for updates." He turned her phone over in his hands to power it down.

She snatched it from him. "At least let me copy my important contacts down. It's not like one minute will matter if they've already got us pinged."

Her words slid ice down his spine. He should've thought of that earlier. Hopefully Rafe's scrambling of their phones worked. He wouldn't take any chances. He strapped on a holster around his ankle and a hidden knife sheath on both forearms.

"Okay, Rambo, is all that necessary?" She tossed her phone into his bag and crossed her arms.

"Well, these guys are willing to blow up an innocent woman to get to you. So, yeah, I think it's necessary." He looked up from tightening the last strap on his arm just in time to see her chest heave. He was such a jerk.

"Can we eat now?" She cocked her eyebrow.

"Come on. Let's go."

He held out his hand, and she tentatively placed her shaking palm in his. His fingers tingled with the contact like he'd connected wires wrong on an electrical manifold. The compact room shrunk in on him. He threaded his fingers with hers and squeezed her hand.

"You stay close to me, right on my side like glue, okay? Remember, we're a happy couple."

She nodded, and he pulled her to the door. They strode casually down the street, his heart thumping in his throat. He couldn't tell if it pumped hard from the possibility of a threat lurking around the corner or how right it felt with Reagan close. Either way, both possibilities were dangerous.

THE NEXT MORNING, Sosimo scanned the car dealer lot, looking for a vehicle to travel across country in. He'd called Cooper the night before to let him know they wouldn't make it to Amarillo until the morning. Hopefully, car shopping wouldn't take long.

He pulled his jacket tighter around him in the chilly autumn air. It probably didn't matter what they got, but he wanted something that wouldn't put him in a worse mood. Too bad his crankiness lay firmly on his shoulders.

Lying awake all night, watching Reagan sleep, worrying about keeping her safe, hadn't done him any favors. Not with how her long braid had snaked over her shoulder, tempting him to unwind it and run his fingers through her hair. There he went again, contemplating things he should leave alone. He scowled as he surveyed the cars before him, finding nothing that he wanted to spend countless hours in.

"What about that?" Reagan grabbed his hand and pointed toward the back of the lot. "Come on. Let's check it out."

He dragged his feet as her fingers tugged on his. She glanced back, her eyes laughing at him as she cocked an eyebrow. He stepped up next to her and threaded his fingers through hers, his skin tingling at every touch point. Though taking her hand was all part of their cover, it seemed so natural now. She stopped in front of a small motorhome.

"It's perfect." She leaned into him. "What do you think?"

He couldn't think, not with her so close. She smelled of maple syrup from breakfast and warmth. She glanced up at him and tipped her head toward the motorhome.

He lifted his free hand and ran his fingers over the silky twists of her braid. Her lips opened slightly, drawing his attention to their full shape. His mind screamed danger, but he couldn't convince himself to care. He didn't have an aversion to danger anyway.

"I see you've found the gem of the lot," a jovial voice said.

Reagan jumped away from Sosimo, her face pinking as she averted her eyes. He flexed his fingers, missing the connection of her. The glare he sent the salesman's way didn't seem to faze the older man.

"This beaut just came in and probably won't last long with all the camping fanatics this area has." The man held out his hand, and Sosimo gripped it. "Bill Landry, at your service."

"John, and my wife, Sue." Why didn't those words upset him as much as they had when Rafe first showed him their fake IDs?

She darted a glance his way before shaking Bill's outstretched hand. "Nice to meet you."

"Now this here Winnebago View is just about perfect for a young couple like yourselves." Bill walked up to the RV and tapped it. "Small and compact, it'll be easy to drive, and you can park this baby just about anywhere. You don't have kids, do you? It's a mite small if you do."

"No kids." Reagan cleared her throat.

What would their kids look like? Would they have her red hair and his dark eyes? His mother would go loco over Reagan, fussing at how bonita she was. What would Reagan think of his family? He shook his head. Dangerous, indeed.

"Newlyweds. I could tell the minute I saw you." Bill clapped his hands and winked. "You'll love the bed. It's perfect for cuddling."

Sosimo inhaled sharply and coughed as he choked on

his spit. Reagan's ears turned red. She crossed her arms. Bill chuckled lightly as he stepped to the RV's door.

"Go ahead and take a peek inside." Bill waved them forward.

Reagan stepped up into the RV, heading toward the back. Sosimo followed her in, turning in the tiny space. It had everything they'd need to lie low. A dinette and galley filled the space next to the door. The bathroom and bedroom were a few steps away in the back. He quickly turned away from the bed, his neck heating, and strode to the driver's seat.

He sat and clenched the steering wheel in his hand. The upscale interior proved a complete contrast to his Ford. Kind of like he and Reagan were opposites.

"This baby has a Mercedes chassis with a turbo-diesel engine. There's a bunk above the seats that can double as storage, and the dinette folds down into a bed. Both seats up front turn to face the living area," Bill yammered on.

It didn't really matter. This was perfect. They could camp their way across the nation, and no one would be the wiser. Maybe they could buy some camp chairs so they wouldn't stay stuck inside the tight space.

"It's low mile—"

"We'll take it," Sosimo interrupted Bill, ready to get back to the hotel to grab their stuff and get on the road.

Twenty minutes later they pulled out of the dealership. It paid to have rich friends. Sosimo dialed the ranch on speaker.

"Sosimo, what's up?" Derrick's deep voice came over the Winnebago's speakers.

"We'll be on the road within a half an hour."

"Got yourself some new wheels?" Derrick's voice held laughter. "Man, didn't I warn you about that old truck? That Ford stands for Found On Road Dead?"

"Funny. You want to come down here and pick up ol' Cinnamon?"

"Not on your life. That truck is more trouble than it's worth."

Reagan laughed next to him. He turned his gaze on her and lifted an eyebrow. She covered her mouth with a hand and looked out her window.

"Tell Zeke we bought the ranch a motorhome. We're hoping it'll help us stay out of sight." Sosimo pulled into the motel parking space and put the vehicle in park. "We're grabbing our gear from the hotel, then heading into Amarillo to pick up Cooper."

"The RV is a brilliant idea. Good thinking," Derrick commented.

Reagan turned to Sosimo.

"Yeah, well, Reagan is supposedly a genius, right?" Sosimo winked at her.

She swatted him on the arm and got out. The sun glinted off her hair, making it look like flames. He swallowed, needing to finish this conversation so she wasn't out there alone. It had everything to do with the people still after her, and nothing to do with the emptiness her absence created. *Liar*.

"Gotta go, D. We'll touch base later." He hung up and climbed out of the RV, trying to keep his gait slow and measured but failing.

He caught up to her as she turned the hotel door and

pushed it open. His heart skipped a beat, and his skin tingled. He pulled her in the room, slammed the door shut, then blocked her behind his back while he scanned the small area. Today, he thanked God he could see every inch of the place, including the bathroom where the tight quarters had been torture the night before. How would he survive traveling in the RV?

"Sos?" She placed her hands on his back and gently pushed, the pressure heating his entire body.

He turned and leaned into her. "Stay close to me."

She pressed against the door, her hands spreading across his chest. "Okay."

He moved closer. "I can't protect you if I can't reach you."

She jerked her hands back, and a forced laugh chopped from her. "Yeah, right. Your job." She averted her gaze. "Well, I guess we better get going. Don't want to make your friend Cooper to keep waiting in Amarillo for us."

She stepped around him, snatched her bag from her bed, and hugged it tight in front of her. She was right. They needed to get going before he did something stupid —like press her up against the door and give in to the need to kiss her.

SEVEN

As they drove through Arkansas later that day, June peered at the lump snoring on the bed in the back of the RV. She had been hesitant to meet Cooper Ford, Sosimo's friend and now sidekick, when she and Sosimo had arrived in Amarillo to pick him up. She shouldn't have fretted. Having the Marine around had proved a great diversion from her mind's need to short circuit whenever she was alone with Sosimo.

After several hours of playing cards with Cooper while Sosimo drove, Cooper had claimed he needed a nap and crashed onto the bed. She wasn't exactly sure how his tall frame could fit comfortably on the short bed, but he'd been sound asleep since. She liked the easy manner the quiet man had, though now that he snoozed in the back, she had to try twice as hard to keep her little crush on Hot Tamale Sosimo under wraps.

She turned back to her computer and clicked her track pad, leaning in to look at her screen more closely.

Not that it would help her current dilemma of figuring out just what exactly didn't work with her body armor invention. Something about the integrated diagnostics didn't react to the soldier's biometrics properly, and she couldn't figure out where she'd messed up. The RV swerved, and she grabbed her computer to keep it from sliding off her lap. She glanced out the front windshield, and when no animal scampered there, she looked over at Sosimo.

"Sorry about that." Sosimo peeked over at her with a chagrined look on his face. "Jackrabbit raced out, and I didn't want to hit it."

Instances like that kept her guessing about Sosimo. She shrugged and slammed the computer closed. "It's all right. I needed to stop staring at the same screen for a while."

"Having troubles?"

"You could say that." June reached back and put the computer on the dinette bench, peeking toward the bed where Cooper slept. "Having troub—"

The ringing of Sosimo's phone interrupted her. He threw her an apologetic glance before pushing the button on the dash to answer the phone call.

"Rafe, what you got for us?" Sosimo asked as he looked in his side mirror and turned on his blinker to pass a car driving slowly.

She loved the route they'd taken so far, trekking across the slow, rolling hills of the Oklahoma plains that transitioned to the beautiful Ozarks of Arkansas. Granted, it had only been one day so far, but she enjoyed country she'd never seen before.

"Sos, you gotta call your mom, man," Rafe moaned over the phone. "She's reached her limit of her precious chico not calling her."

June placed her feet on the dash and laid her arms on her legs. She couldn't imagine Sosimo as a precious boy.

Sosimo rolled his eyes. "I just talked to her last week. I'll call her when I can. She has other kids she can harp on."

"I thought you'd say that." Rafe's voice held a hint of teasing to it. "I've been holding her off for days. It's time for you to talk to her. I'm patching her through right now."

"Ay, caraye. Wait, Rafe—"

"Mijo, is that you?" a hesitant voice said on the other line.

"Sí, Mama, it's me," Sosimo answered, gripping his neck with his hand and peeking over at June.

An excited squeal was followed by rapid words too fast to believe someone spoke. June could tell by the tone in Sosimo's mother's voice that she loved talking to him. He answered the questions in just as rapid Spanish, glancing over at her and mouthing, "Sorry." When his mother continued talking quickly, June stared at him in fascination. She'd grown up all around the world but had never experienced such obvious joy in one another as she did with this conversation.

During the call, the phone got put on speaker by his family. So many voices rattled off words in rapid succession that she didn't even know how Sosimo kept it all straight. Sosimo laughed, contentment on his face as he answered whatever had just been said. June peeked back toward Cooper, amazed the man could still be sleeping.

She turned forward, staring out the window at the Arkansas Ozarks that lined the road. Had she ever felt that connection in her own family? Definitely not since her brother had died. She didn't even think before he'd died either. Her father had always said he wanted to explore the world they were fortunate enough to be stationed in. He hadn't wanted to waste time visiting the world he already knew. Because of that, she never really got to know her cousins. Never really knew her grandparents before they all died. Then, after her brother's death, and it was just three of them, the world became even lonelier.

Sosimo sighed as the phone call ended and glanced over at her. "I'm really sorry about that. Rafe loves to razz us any chance he can get."

June pasted on a smile and peeked over at him. "That's okay. You sound like you have a wonderful family."

He shrugged, but his enormous smile negated the casual action. "They're a handful. Well ... more than handful, actually, but I love them. My mom threatened Rafe that she wouldn't make him pabellón criollo next time he comes to visit." He shook his head, humor in his voice. "It's a good thing he never got captured and interrogated by terrorists."

"I'm sure Rafe would've done just fine." June turned her attention out the windshield. She saw Sosimo peek at her from the corner of her eye. His eyebrow winged up.

"Yeah, you're probably right. My mom's much worse than fundamental terrorists."

She gasped. "If I ever meet her, I'll tell her you said so."

His head cocked to one side, and his eyes narrowed. "You wouldn't dare."

"No, probably not. I'd be in such awe, I most likely wouldn't say a word." She chuckled as she reached for her box of Mike and Ike's. "Or I might freeze in fear with my back to a corner. They sound very intimidating."

"Nah, just loud and numerous."

June leaned her head back against the headrest, pulled her knees up to her chest, and sighed. "That must've been amazing, living in a large family like that."

"It had its goods and bads. Mostly it was good." His lips lifted on one side.

"How many siblings do you have?" She turned sideways in the seat so she could watch him.

"Ten."

She coughed, placing her hand over her mouth so her fruity candy didn't fly out and pelt him. Why'd she have to put so many in her mouth at once? Ten kids ... that sounded crazy and wonderful. Would she have even survived?

"You okay?" He placed his hand on her knee.

Lightning shot up her leg, and she almost swallowed the mass of candies whole. The RV heaved on a bump in the road, causing Sosimo to grip the steering wheel again. Her leg tingled with his lingering energy. She swallowed the last of the deathly candies and clunked the box in the cup holder. He raised his eyebrow at her before turning his attention back to the bumpy road.

"I'm good. You just caught me off guard with your army-sized family." She leaned forward, glad they'd purchased the RV so she could move more freely. "What was it like? Where were you in the lineup? Was your house crowded? Did you fight all the time?"

Sosimo tipped his head back and laughed, a deep, wonderful sound that shot those lingering tingles on her leg straight to her belly. "It was great and horrible at the same time. I'm the third kid. My father is one of the best orthopedic surgeons in Florida. When I was younger, the house was smaller, but my parents kept moving to accommodate the kids they kept popping out." His smile turned soft. "Though, my mom hasn't let my dad move her in the last fifteen years. Claims she enjoys having her family close and a bigger house will put too much distance between them."

"I can see that."

"Fighting was a given. You squeeze a bunch of passionate Venezuelans in a house and things are bound to get hot." He winked at her, and she intimately understood as heat filled her core.

"So your mom must be a marvelous cook if Rafe would throw you under the bus for a meal."

"The best. Better than any place I've ever eaten." He pointed at her. "And I'm not just saying that because she's my mom. It's her passion, her gift. She says food is the language of the soul, and she's the translator."

Reagan sighed. "That's beautiful."

"I used to sit in the kitchen for hours, helping her just so I might one day be able to cook even half as good as she does. The house always smells delicious. Always. I had to join the Army just so I didn't end up weighing two hundred pounds."

"Yeah, right?" She tapped him on the shoulder. "Why did you join?"

He stilled. The absence of animated expressions on his face was instantaneous. Shoot. Her stomach bottomed out, and her throat thickened.

"I'm sorry. I'm prying."

"No. It's okay."

He inhaled, held it for a second, then let it out. His gaze ping-ponged from her back to the road. He closed his eyes for a moment before pulling his shoulders back.

"It was just about the only option for a knucklehead like me."

"Wha—I don't understand."

"My family is full of smart people. Smart like you." He shrugged. "I'm not like my family."

"That's not true." Her voice sounded strangled as she denied what he said.

"Yeah, yeah it is." He tapped his thumb on the steering wheel. "I struggled in school. Man, did I struggle. Found out later that I have severe dyslexia. Most of my teachers just thought I was stupid and lazy, would never amount to anything."

Reagan gasped. "They told you that?"

"Some did, others just gave up after a month or two. My fifth grade teacher didn't though. Mr. Thomas. He's the one who realized the words and letters like to dance around on me." He grinned as he shook his head. "Even knowing, I still struggled through school. Barely graduated. But I enjoyed Rifle Club and tinkering with engines. College was definitely out of the question. My junior year, after getting in-school suspension again, my dad said my need to protect others might be useful in the Army."

"Protect others?"

His forehead scrunched as he grimaced. "In elementary school, I hated seeing kids get picked on. I got enough of that myself. I guess I figured that if I couldn't be smart, I had to be something, so I protected others from bullies. Stepped in when they couldn't."

"I can see that. Sosimo, the hero." She twisted her hands together to keep from reaching out.

"More like Sosimo, the troublemaker." He shook his head. "I spent more time in detention than I did class, I think."

"I bet it broke your mother's heart to have you enlist. Not having you there in the kitchen with her anymore."

"She has nine others who've stuck close to home. She lived." He pulled up to the Village Creek State Park kiosk and paid the attendant for a campsite.

She laughed, shaking her head. This man amazed her. Nothing like any of the other men she'd known on base or after. His life was so different from hers that she wished she could just step out of hers and cling to his. Her cheeks flushed, and her heart rate picked up. He rolled the window back up and put the RV in drive.

She threw caution out the window, leaned forward,

and kissed him on the cheek. "Thanks for sharing with me."

He glanced at her and swallowed. "You're welcome." His voice came out deeper than normal.

She settled back in her seat with a sigh, trying to hide her embarrassment. "What I wouldn't give to live in a family like that."

"What's your family like?"

Nuts. She walked right into that one. She turned her legs forward and put her feet on the dash. She'd have to be careful. She couldn't slip about her father. Not if she wanted him to like her for herself.

She peeked at Sosimo. He would be different, though. She could sense that, but the life she'd built depended on her family staying a secret to some extent.

"I've always been introverted, painfully so when I was younger. Still so, actually." She picked at some lint on her pants. "I was the oddball, probably would've been someone you would've been protecting. When other girls were playing dress-up and dolls, I was taking apart circuit boards and studying molecular structure. My dad would get into huffs about why I didn't have friends like my brother. Why did I hole myself up in my room when the base was full of other girls to play with? It didn't help that the base was different every few years."

She reached for the box of candy. The fruitiness sweetened the bitter memories. She peeked over at Sosimo, and he nodded in encouragement.

"I started begging to be homeschooled around fourth grade. It wasn't until my brother died when I was fourteen that my parents finally agreed."

"How'd he die?"

"Motorcycle accident two months after he turned sixteen."

Sosimo winced and placed his hand on her shoulder. "I'm sorry."

"Thanks." She shrugged, glad the weight of grief had eased over the years. "Our already quiet house became painfully silent. Still is reserved. Reserved and orderly." She mock saluted. Relaxing her head back against the seat, she closed her eyes. "That's why your family sounds amazing and scary and something I'll probably never have the pleasure of experiencing."

Wow. How pathetic did her voice sound right now? She cleared her throat and shook out some more candies.

"When did you start inventing things?" Sosimo smiled knowingly at her.

She grabbed on to the lifeline with relish. "When I was nine, I started testing things. I had a lot of gadgets fail miserably. Still do. The one you call Superman was the first thing worth making public, though my mom swears I should patent the clothes steamer I made for her."

"What's that?"

"It's kind of like an extra-long garment bag that she puts her clothes in, pushes a button, and walks away. She says she likes how she can go put her face on and her clothes are wrinkle free when she's done."

He chuckled as he turned off the main park road. "Seems like something my mom would like. Can I special order one? You'll make me son of the year. That's difficult to do with six of us."

She laughed. "From the sounds of it, you just show

up and you'll earn that spot on your own." She shrugged as he drove through the tree-lined park, glad they'd decided on staying here rather than a campground off the highway. "I could whip her up one. I kind of owe it to you after all I've put you through."

"You don't owe me a thing. I'm glad I can help." His voice had an insistence to it that made her believe he truly meant it.

He pulled the RV into an empty spot and threw the vehicle in park. He stretched out his neck as he unbuckled. Well, show and tell time ended.

She pressed her buckle free and lifted the armrest to escape the revealing conversation. She swung her legs between the seats to stand but stopped when he placed a hand on her shoulder. His thumb rubbed up and down her neck, short-circuiting her brain cells. He leaned close, his spicy scent intoxicating her. She tried to breathe it in deep, take it into her very essence, but her tight lungs constricted her airflow.

He stopped his approach a mere inch from her lips. Would he kiss her? She held her breath.

"Thanks for sharing with me." He kissed her on the cheek, right on the corner of her lips.

Her heart shrank. "You're welcome." She squeezed the words out.

Thank goodness she hadn't turned to meet his lips, though part of her wanted to grab his head and make him kiss her right. He opened the driver's door and said something about claiming their spot.

At least she thought he said that.

His voice sounded muffled against the blood rushing in her ears.

The door snapped shut, causing her to jump. She'd better get up and move. It'd only emphasize her pathetic nature if she still sat in a daze when he returned.

She stood on shaky legs, clutching the front of her shirt that seemed tight. Ay, caray. She was in trouble.

EIGHT

"What are you doing?" Sosimo muttered as he took the campground ticket and clipped it to the site number. Why in the world had he almost kissed Reagan? He raked his hand through his hair. He knew why. Even a knucklehead like himself could sense the way they'd bonded.

He couldn't deny that his thoughts about her had changed. She wasn't just some rich socialite raising money for the poor soldiers. She'd been through it. He knew the stress of moving from base to base, especially when he had a hard time making friends to begin with. He'd been fortunate going from his enormous family to the family within his team. He couldn't imagine what it would've been like to grow up so alone.

He peered around the campsite. With it being the middle of the week and autumn, they practically had the entire campground to themselves. He took a deep breath, cleansing his nose of her inviting scent with the musty smell of dry leaves.

Maybe they needed to get out of the RV. They had been traveling for over twelve hours. He just needed to wake up his brain so he could keep from doing something they'd both regret. Like having Cooper catch Sosimo kissing the daylights out of her.

He marched up to the side door and snapped it open. "I'm going for a walk. Want to come?"

Reagan, who was attempting to open a bag of chips, jumped, ripping the bag open. Chips flew to all corners of the RV. She stared wide-eyed at him for a second before her face turned red. He burst out laughing.

"You scared the daylights out of me." She glanced around the RV at the chips now covering all the flat surfaces. Her eyes closed to slits as she turned her gaze back to him. She pointed a finger toward his face. "You're helping me clean this up."

"Okay, but we're taking a walk first." He stepped to the door and leaned in to holler to Cooper. "Coop, we're going for a walk."

"All right, give me a sec, and I'll be ready," Cooper's groggy voice mumbled from the back.

"Don't worry about it. Nothing here but the birds in the trees." Sosimo stepped back and motioned for Reagan to follow.

She grabbed a handful of chips from the bag and set the torn thing on the table before she carefully stepped her way out of the RV. She looked adorable as she attempted to not crush the chips as she tiptoed out of the RV. When she got outside, she extended a chip toward him. Generosity was threaded through the very fabric of her being.

"Does Cooper normally sleep that much?" She popped a chip into her mouth.

Sosimo shrugged. "He's taking the night shift tonight. He's just getting as much sleep as he can so he doesn't get tired later."

"You and your night shifts, poor guy." She smirked and turned in a circle. "Look how beautiful it is out here."

Her expression held a sense of awe, like the night before at the Blue Swallow Motel. Did she always approach life with such wonder, or was she just so far out of her norm that she couldn't help it? Whatever the case, what would it be like to be the one she experienced life with? If she was truly as shy as she said she was, there'd be a lot of life she hadn't experienced yet. Warmth spread through his chest as he glanced over at her in the dimming evening light. He shook off the thought and marched through the grass toward the lake at a fast clip.

"I wish we would've gotten here earlier. We could've hiked around the lake." Reagan brushed off her hands and shaded her eyes as she glanced up at the retreating sun. She brought her hand down, lifting her eyebrows at him in question. "Think we have time to trek down the way a little?"

"Sure."

He'd been watching their tail all day. He didn't doubt that the people after Reagan might eventually catch up to them. For now, they were still safe.

A bird twittered and swooped over the lake. Reagan pointed to it, but his attention stayed glued to her. The dimming evening sun made her hair a richer tone of red where it curled around her face and down her back. He liked her like this—relaxed, dressed in leggings and a long shirt. Not that he didn't find her attractive in her formal wear. Then she'd been gorgeous. Now, she was awe-inspiring.

"So ... what are you making us for dinner?" Reagan asked as she pulled a yellow leaf from a low-hanging branch.

Sosimo shook his head to focus. "What?"

"Well, you told me you spent countless hours helping your sweet mom. I figured you'd feed us." Reagan tossed the leaf at him. "I'm not sure if you noticed, but my only contribution to the shopping cart of groceries was from the candy and chip aisle."

He laughed. "Is that all you ever eat?"

"No. I'm also proficient at bowls of cereal and microwave meals." She plucked another leaf down. "They've really improved the freezer section over the last several years." She tossed the leaf at him again, and he cocked his eyebrow at her playfulness. "When I'm home, I use this great service that delivers premade home-cooked meals for me. All I have to do is warm them up."

"I'll whip us up something when we get back."

"It better be good. I'm starving."

"When are you not?"

"When I'm in the zone. Speaking of, we need to go by my house tomorrow when we drive through Tennessee. I need to pick up the prototype and some equipment to try to figure out my glitch before we get to Virginia."

"I thought your homes were in Maryland and

Texas?" They'd been the only residences they could find for her.

"The place in Maryland I keep for when I'm visiting my parents." She kicked at the dried leaves on the grass. "I'm not real fond of staying with them. Quick visits are great. Long ones, not so much."

"Hmm."

"The house in Texas is where I stay when I'm setting up the inventions with my testing lab and manufacturing facility there."

"Where do we have to go then?"

"It's not far, only about three hours from here. It's in a little town called Paris, Tennessee." She grabbed a strip of her hair and twisted it in her hand. "I thought we could plan on staying there tomorrow. That would give me time to round everything up and maybe run another diagnostic through my computer in the lab."

"Paris, huh?" He'd have to ask Rafe to look into her house.

"Yeah, they've even built a replica of the Eiffel Tower." She shook her head. "It was less the name of the town and more the isolation of it that drew me. I'm still only two hours from the Memphis airport, but my nearest neighbor is a mile away through thick forest. I set up security to keep my stuff safe when I'm gone, but no one will look in backwoods Tennessee for me. It's not a place where I spend a lot of time."

"What isn't?"

"The outdoors." She motioned her arms around her. "Remember, I'm a geek who spends far too much time in her lab."

"So why all the secrecy? Why not just live in Texas where your other lab is?" He studied her closely, wishing the fading light didn't put so much of her face in shadows.

"Paranoia?" Her laugh sounded forced. She sighed and stopped, staring absently over the lake. "When I almost had the Superman done, I trusted the wrong person. We had been dating for about a year. He kept hinting at marriage. He ... well, he tried to steal my invention and sell it as his own."

He touched the back of her hand. "I'm sorry."

"Yeah, well, story of my life. Guys are only ever interested when I can advance their career. I should've known better." She had a hardness in her voice he didn't like.

He definitely couldn't care less what she could do for him. Something about her called to him. She continued along the lakeside, kicking a little more violently at the leaves than before. A rustling in the brushes pulled her up short, and Sosimo lengthened his strides to catch up to her. From the sound of it, it was most likely a small animal that had ventured to the water to drink, but he bet she didn't know that.

"Is it a bear?" She reached out to him, fumbling with finding his arm since she wouldn't take her eyes off the bushes.

"Maybe." He couldn't help the concerned whisper and leaning closer.

"We ... we should go back." Her voice was so low he almost didn't hear it.

"Probably." He stifled his laughter.

He stepped closer, thanking the little critter for

creating the perfect opportunity to offer security without worry of being shot or blown up. Mid-step toward her, a raccoon sauntered out from under the bush. Reagan shrieked, stumbling backward and knocking into him. He backpedaled, tripping over a downed branch. Arms flapping, he barely registered Reagan's mouth falling open before the frigid lake water slapped his back and wrapped his body completely.

When he surfaced, sputtering, Reagan stood on the edge of the lake, her hands covering her mouth. A quick scan proved the devious trash bandit had scurried away. Sosimo stood and slugged out of the lake, shaking the water off.

"I'm so sorry." She touched his shoulder, yanking it back to her side. "I didn't know you were so close."

So much for offering her protection.

"I knew he was there, but he just popped out like he was after us." Her hand shook as she lifted it to her chest.

The critter had done no such thing, but Sos let it slide. He thought of her face as he'd fallen and wondered what he must have looked like. The whole situation had laughter bubbling up his chest. His chuckle died in his throat as she stared at his shirt clinging to his body. He swallowed and cleared his throat.

She cringed. "You're soaking wet."

"Want a hug?" He held his dripping arms out.

She backed up laughing, her hands up in front of her to ward him off. "No, no, thank you. Maybe later." Her eyes widened before she ducked her head and turned toward the RV. "Might as well head back. I have a mess to clean up, and you need to change so you can feed me."

She jogged toward the campsite. He shivered. His cold clothes clung to his skin, erasing the heat that had spread through him with her slipped confession. He walked back, allowing time to gather his thoughts. When he got back, the door to the Winnebago sat open, the shower in the teeny bathroom ran, and Reagan kneeled, using her hands to sweep the chips into a pile.

"Wait, don't come in. There's no broom here, and your dripping clothes will just make a bigger mess." She stood, pushing her hair out of her face. "Let me grab you some dry clothes."

"What, you want me to strip out here?" Sosimo gaped at her.

She leaned out the door and scanned the area. "Who are you worried about seeing you? The raccoons?"

He glanced around, remembering that the only other campers had been on the other side of the campground. He could always tuck behind the camper if need be.

"Just grab whatever is on the top of my bag for me."

He moved toward the picnic table, pulling off the soaking shirt. He tossed it onto the tabletop and stretched his muscles that ached from the hours on the road and the massive bruise he still sported from the attack in Aspen. A gasp whirled him around, and he almost knocked into Reagan.

"Your back." She pushed on his shoulder, forcing him to face the table. "It looks horrible."

Her fingers skimmed over the tender spot where the bullet had hit his body armor. He closed his eyes to the trail of fire that lit him like a sparkler, sparks flying this way and that. Her fingers shook as a trembling gulp sounded behind him. He turned, her fingers sliding around his side until he faced her. She dropped her hand, averting her gaze.

He grabbed her hand. "Reagan?"

The tears that shone in her eyes when she dragged her gaze back to him gripped his heart in a vice.

She bit her lip and ducked her head. "I'm sorry, Sosimo. It's my fault you're so hurt."

"No." The word rushed out, causing her to flinch.

"It is. If I would've taken the threat seriously—" She shook her head, her shoulders drawing up and her elbows tucking tight into her sides. "You could've died."

He grabbed her arms. "But I didn't."

She covered her face with her hands. "Maybe I'm doing this all wrong. Maybe I'm just making things worse. I mean, if soldiers aren't even getting the units I'm sending out there for them, what's the point of all this?"

He pulled her close, wrapping his arms around her. "You're helping, Reagan. Helping a lot. Not only the soldiers out in the field, but those that need help after. Without your invention, we would lose a lot more lives."

She placed her forehead on his collarbone. "I just keep wondering where those extra units went? Now all of this fiasco over my invention makes me worried they're all getting in the wrong hands somehow. Then Zeke and you get shot. The nanny's car blows up." She lifted her face, her gaze questioning. "What if it's me? What if I'm so focused on making this work that I'm being an idiot?"

"Ay, cariña, it's not you." He wrapped his arms tighter around her, tucking his face into her hair. "We live in a world that's full of evil—a darkness pushing against what's light and good. We try to do our part to keep it at bay. That's what you're doing. Battling against the dark, equipping those who need help in the fight."

She lifted her head and stared into his eyes. The smell of fruity candies still lingered on her. She pressed her trembling hands against his chest and slowly rose on the balls of her feet. Her lips brushed against his, soft and fluttery like butterfly wings. She pulled back an inch before leaning forward and lightly kissing him again. She hugged him with a soft, "Thank you."

She spun away and rushed to the RV. An icy breeze replaced the warmth of her, causing Sosimo to shiver. He'd been hesitant about this assignment, but not anymore. He rubbed the back of his fingers across his lips as he smiled. In fact, this may just end up the best assignment of his life.

NINE

June still couldn't believe that she'd kissed Sosimo the night before. She'd tried to pretend like it hadn't happened, that she hadn't thrown all her inhibitions out the window and kissed the most amazing man she'd ever met—a man so unlike her father she wondered how she ever could've compared them. It didn't work. The tension between them was thick as taffy. Her mind wanted to think of nothing but that brief kiss and his heartwarming words. It made it really hard to focus on what she'd brought them to her home to do.

She shifted from one foot to the other as she bent over her computers, pulling up data and analyzing it as quickly as she could. She had a program running to pull all her information from the hard drive and transfer it to the external memory she planned on taking with her. The recent attacks may have left her a little paranoid. She'd never wiped her computer clean in the past, but if whoever was after her found this place, she didn't want to leave her inventions to chance.

"I love your home. Very chevere." Sosimo strutted down the stairs, taking a large bite out of an apple. "Cooper's upstairs keeping an eye on things. I wanted to see if you need anything. You've been holed up down here a long time."

He wiped the juice off of his chin with his sleeve. Her stomach growled. She'd forgotten to eat lunch again. She glanced at the empty box of Hot Tamales she'd polished off a few minutes ago, knowing that didn't count as a meal.

"I need your help." She motioned him over. "First off, I need a bite of that."

She leaned over while typing and opened her mouth. His deep chuckle swirled in her gut. He held the apple up to her waiting mouth. She took a large bite, rubbing her mouth on her shoulder to catch the juice.

"Ay, caray. You took half the apple." He held the fruit to his face and examined it.

"What? I'm hungry." She spoke around the massive chunk in her mouth, chewing as fast as she could.

"You've missed ..." Sosimo turned her head to him.

He stared at her lips, her hands stilling on the keyboard. He swallowed. She couldn't breathe, couldn't do anything but stand frozen with her fingers poised over the keys and her heart pounding in her chest. His thumb brushed against her lips, the motion light and hesitant. She licked them, tasting the apple. He blinked a few times, then with excruciating slowness lifted his eyes to hers.

"Second?" His hoarse question had her forehead

wrinkling in what she could only imagine as unattractive confusion. "First, you needed a bite. Second, you need ..."

She straightened, shaking the moment out of her brain. "Right. I need you to try this on so I can run some diagnostics."

She closed the computer program and disconnected the suit from the cord. Shaking it out, she handed it to him. He held it up, turning it left and right. The apple soured in her stomach, the anticipation of what he'd think building until she worried she'd spew apple chunks everywhere. Stupid nerves.

"Um ...this is it?" His voice held a concerned tone. "It looks like a speed skating outfit, not armor."

June reached for it, then pulled her hands back. "That was the idea. I wanted something that was light-weight that wouldn't hinder movement. I synthetically engineered spider silk, then combined it with Dyneema and graphene to create a fabric that is both flexible and practically impenetrable." She forced herself to stop talking.

He stretched the material and held it up to him. "Will it fit?"

Her nervous giggle made her cringe. "It's designed to stretch and meld to any body type."

"Chevere. Cool." He smiled at her, his expression warm with pride. "You're amazing."

He winked and strode toward the bathroom. June leaned against her high desk and fanned herself. He would be the death of her, one sexy look at a time. She turned back to the computer screens and checked the status on the transfer. It flashed complete on the screen, so she ejected the external hard drive and placed it in her backpack with the rest of the gear she'd collected. Now, she just needed to run diagnostics on the suit itself and throw her laptop in the pack.

The door to the bathroom opened, drawing her attention to Sosimo as he strutted out, tossing his clothes on the desk.

"I pulled my pants over the top." He grimaced. "I'm confident, but not that confident."

She gulped, amazed at how the suit accentuated every muscle across his chest. He stopped a few feet away, held out his arms, and turned.

"Well, what do you think?" He smoothed his hand down the front of him.

Nice ... very, very nice. She cleared her throat. "The question is, what do you think?"

He moved his body, twisting and punching. "It feels good. I'm not used to everything being this tight, but the fabric doesn't chafe. It's so light, it's almost like I'm not wearing it at all."

"That's ... good," June choked out as she ducked her head to hide her warming cheeks.

She moved around him, lifting his arm, checking the seams, and running her hands along the silky fabric tightly encasing his sculpted body. This would work. Tingling started in her head and rushed to her fingers, sending gooseflesh across her skin. She came back around him, not able to contain the large smile spread across her face.

She touched his collar. "Turn the suit on with the button right here and let's see if I fixed the glitches."

He pressed the button and data streamed through her program. The steady beep-beep of Sosimo's heart beat from her speakers. She clapped and placed her hands on her cheeks that hurt from smiling. Everything left her mind except the rush of excitement that ran warm through her body.

She turned and threw her arms around Sosimo's neck with a squeal. "It's transmitting. I couldn't get it to communicate before."

He lifted her and twirled her in a circle. Joy bubbled out of her as she tipped her head back and laughed. He stopped spinning and lowered her with excruciating slowness. She vaguely registered the beeping of the computer as his heart rate increased. It pounded against her palm she'd flattened against his chest.

He brought his hand up and tucked her hair behind her ear, trailing his fingers along her neck. "Eres increíble."

The beeping sped up even faster, matching the rapid drumming of her own heart. Would he initiate the kiss this time? Should she just kiss him again and risk looking pathetic or pushy or both? Her pulse quickened, and she hoped she didn't pass out.

His smile built slowly as he anchored his arms around her and pulled her tighter against him. If she waited any longer, her brain may just overheat and stop functioning all together. She lifted onto her toes on shaky legs and tentatively pressed her lips to his. They were soft, yet strong, accepting her kiss with an attentiveness that turned her already unstable legs to jelly. She slid her hands up his chest and threaded her fingers through his hair. Every synapse in her body fired at once, threatening to overwhelm her.

"You're driving me crazy," he whispered against her lips before trailing kisses along her cheek and down her neck.

Could kissing make her chest explode? Her back pressed against her desk, and he cradled her head as he claimed her mouth again. Feeling bolder than she'd ever felt before, she playfully dragged her teeth over his lower lip. He growled and deepened the kiss. This was it. She would implode, she was sure of it.

A loud alarm went off on her computer, and Sosimo groaned and chuckled low. "I think we broke your invention, cariña."

"That's not the suit." She exhaled the words as he kissed below her ear. "It's the proximity alarm."

Sosimo stilled, his breath skimming her skin in harsh bursts of air. "What?" He pulled back and his penetrating gaze made her blink.

The fog that the last few minutes had settled over her brain cleared as the alarm fully registered. "The house's proximity alarms."

He moved away as she turned and started pulling up feeds on her computer. Rustling of fabric sounded behind her as one screen after another came up with people sneaking onto her property in the cover of the dark night. She glanced back as Sosimo pulled his shirt over the suit and tightened his belt.

"People are here." Her limbs shook for a whole new reason.

"We've got company!" Cooper hissed down the stairs.

Sosimo stepped up next to her, scanned the feeds, and pointed to an empty screen. "Where's that?"

She leaned close to the screen, her forehead scrunching. "It's near the hayloft at the back of the property."

He bent and tied his shoes. "Okay, can we sneak out a window facing that side?"

"Yeah." She closed her eyes as a rock settled in her stomach.

He cupped her cheek in his palm. The connection kept her from dissolving.

"Reagan, look at me." His eyes were fierce when she finally opened hers. "I'll get you out of here." He kissed her—a desperate kiss that left her weak and bolstered at the same time. "Grab your stuff. We have to go."

She nodded, turning back to her laptop and shoving it into her backpack. She swung it onto her back, then started typing on her home computer. A few keystrokes later, the computer counted backwards a program that would destroy the computer system, keeping anything that she had missed from the intruders. She rushed after Sosimo, who scanned the family room at the top of the stairs.

Never had her lab felt as confining as it did at that moment. *Oh, please, please, please let me live.* She didn't want to die, not when the most amazing man just gave her a reason to stop hiding in her lab and experience life among the living.

SOSIMO SHOOK the last of the residual fuzz from his brain. He needed complete focus and couldn't think about kissing Reagan. She stepped up below him on the stairs, looking at her phone screen. She shook her head just as the front doorknob jiggled.

"It's not good. They've circled too fast." Lines formed on her forehead. "We need a diversion."

"I'll draw their attention, while you and Cooper go out the back. Hide in the woods until I find you." If he made it. He left that detail out.

"You're an idiot if you think I'm letting you do that." She shoved the phone in her jacket pocket and zipped it closed. "I have an idea."

She raced back down the stairs, and Sosimo growled, adjusting the pack on his back. She rushed back up the stairs and handed him a heavy box as she passed.

"Get this opened. I'll be right back." She hurried to the back of the house before he could stop her.

She would be the death of him. He glanced at the box, a smile growing as he realized her plan. He pulled out his knife as he crossed the room and set the box on the coffee table.

"Reagan said to help you." Cooper rushed into the room and skidded to a halt, a low whistle coming from his lips. "That's a heck of a lot of Tannerite."

"Yeah." Sosimo cut into the first container. "She had it in her lab."

"She's one special woman, that's for sure." Cooper grabbed a box and worked on opening it.

"That she is." Sosimo tried not to let Cooper's words flare his jealousy.

Reagan came back into the room with a large protein powder container that had to hold over a gallon and a propane tank from a grill. "Will this be big enough?"

"Yeah." Sosimo pointed to the propane and cocked his eyebrow.

She shrugged. "I keep it inside the back entryway so it doesn't walk off while I'm gone."

"You realize this will destroy your house, right?" Cooper looked at her as he passed her a container of Tannerite.

"Hopefully it disorients them long enough for us to get out." She squeezed the bridge of her nose before lifting her eyes to Cooper then Sosimo. "How did they find us? No one but my parents know about this place." She shook her head and started unscrewing the container.

They worked quickly and had the container full in a matter of seconds. Cooper led Reagan to the back of the house as Sosimo put on the lid and shook the homemade bomb as he walked to the front door. He placed the Tannerite up against the door, then put the propane tank in front of that. *Please let this work.* He jiggled the handle to get the people on the other side to focus on the door. He rushed to the back of the house where Reagan stood beside Cooper who peeked out the window.

Sosimo shook his muscles loose and aimed for the container. He shot and dove into the bedroom as a deafening explosion shook the house.

"They're leaving." Cooper opened the window and ducked out.

Scrambling to his feet, Sosimo dashed to the exit. Screams and hollering sounded from the front of the house. It wouldn't take them long to reorganize.

He shook his head to stop the ringing in his ears and helped Reagan out the window. He jumped out after her and pulled her close, running a hand across her cheek, the light leaking through the curtains showing her frightened face.

"¿Estás bien?"

She nodded. He grabbed her hand and took off for the woods with Cooper covering their six. An impact punched Sosimo's side as the echo of the shot hit his ears. Crap.

Cooper returned two quick shots. "Clear."

Sosimo pushed harder, forcing his legs to hurry. They burst through the forest just as a shout sounded from the house.

He didn't stop, just kept pushing over fallen trees and brush. When they got close to the barn where they'd parked the RV, he pulled her down to crouch next to him. He gritted his teeth. Men swarmed the barn with all the lights on, making it impossible to get to their vehicle. Probably for the best, though the enemy would have all the gear he hadn't taken to the house. A Winnebago didn't make for the best getaway car.

He pulled Reagan close and whispered low. "How far is your closest neighbor?"

She turned her head, her lips brushing his ear as she spoke. "A mile through the woods that way."

She pulled back and pointed through the woods behind them past Cooper who had crouched, covering the way they'd just come from. They'd have to move fast if they wanted to beat these guys there. Sosimo picked his way through the trees, trying to make as little noise as possible.

As they got farther away, he increased their pace, rushing through the darkened woods at a reckless speed. Reagan grunted and stumbled but kept up. When he crossed a worn trail cutting through the forest, he took a chance, pulled his sidearm out of the holster, and followed the wooded path. Two minutes later they crouched in the woods, staring at the black house.

"I don't see anyone." Her words came out choppy.

"Me neither."

He rubbed the back of his neck, the tension in his stomach knotting it tight. Without involving the neighbor, they had limited choices.

Cooper pointed toward the garage. "We take the motorcycles."

Sosimo felt slightly bad for stealing. "We'll roll them out to the road so the neighbors don't wake up. Hopefully, it'll be morning before they realize they're missing. Thankfully, I have the cash, our cards, and IDs in my pack."

She nodded, drawing his gaze to the blood on her cheek. His heart raced as he rubbed his thumb along her jaw. Her stumble in the woods suddenly made sense.

"Oh, cariña."

"It's nothing." She turned her determined gaze to him. "I'm fine."

Her eyes blazed. She was furious and more beautiful than anyone he'd ever seen. He had to get her to safety. Then he would think about the emotions swirling through his brain—thoughts of introducing her to his madre and transforming one of the unused cabins at the ranch to a secure lab.

He leaned forward and gave her a quick kiss. "Let's go."

He scanned the area one last time, then followed Cooper into the yard. When no shots rang out, they sprinted to the motorcycles, and he tied his pack to the back. Reagan grabbed his sidearm and turned to cover their six.

"You know how to use that thing?" He grunted as he tightened the bungees the owner had wrapped around the back of the bike.

"How do you think I test my products?" She tossed an annoyed look over her shoulder. "I was shooting guns by the time I was five. You focus on what you're doing. I've got this."

He chuckled as he pushed the machine up the driveway. Trees lining the long walk to the highway hid them. When they got to the road, he leaned the bike on its stand and surveyed the road in both directions.

When all appeared clear, Cooper nodded at Sosimo and he eased out into the road. He climbed onto the seat and hot-wired the bike. After handing him back his gun, Reagan climbed on behind him, wrapping her arms tightly around his body. Maybe they should've gotten a motorcycle to begin with.

He eased on the throttle and sped up down the road.

He really didn't care where they went at this point. She laid her head on his shoulder with a deep exhale he felt heave against his back. He just needed to get her somewhere safe. Then they could figure out what the heck had just happened.

TEN

June stared at her disheveled appearance in the twenty-four-hour diner's bathroom mirror. Her hair spun out in all directions like a nest of fire. The slash across her cheek had dried with blood streaking from it. Why had she even bothered with putting on makeup? Dark circles of smeared mascara highlighted the dark circles left from her exhaustion. It wouldn't surprise her if the cops showed up just based on her looks alone.

She cranked the handle on the paper towel roll, ripped the brown paper with more force than necessary, and got busy fixing her face. The last three hours had passed with horrifying slowness as they made their way to Elizabethtown, Kentucky. Over and over she asked herself how those men could've possibly found them. Every time she came up empty.

Whoever was after her couldn't track her phone. It had been off since they left New Mexico. She had more protection on her computer than the White House, thanks to her paranoia, so it couldn't have been that. The mystery frustrated her beyond belief. It scared her even more than the frustration. How could they hide from people who found the unfindable?

She leaned closer to the mirror and examined her cheek. The cut probably wouldn't scar. What would Sosimo think if it did? People say chicks dig scars, but did guys? She shook her head and worked on taking off her makeup.

The relationship had changed between them and left her exhilarated. He was nothing like the other guys she had met. At the house, he'd never ordered her about, but accepted her help with no question. She inhaled around her expanding heart.

She dug through her pocket for her hair tie and pulled her red nest into a form of ordered chaos. Giving one last nod of confidence to her reflection, she opened the door with a determined yank. She had a man to celebrate with, and she planned to do that celebrating in style.

She found his eyes already trained on her, like he had kept them on the bathroom door the entire time. Vaguely, she realized Cooper wasn't sitting with Sosimo. Sosimo had sat in a booth in the corner where he could both face the door and the bathroom. His phone to his ear, his lips moved rapidly as he talked to whoever was on the other line. His gaze never wavered from her. He stood from the booth when she got close, sliding the phone into his pocket. She stopped before him, her heart banging painfully in her chest.

His head tilted to the side as his eyes narrowed. "Everything okay?"

She nodded and stepped close, pressing her palms to his chest. His eyes widened, but his hands anchored on her hips. She rose up on her toes and pressed her lips to his, lingering as she let out all her tension. Here, she was safe—safe to be herself and embrace life. Here, the awkward science geek faded to a woman cherished. Here was where she wanted to stay, however that looked.

She kissed him quickly two more times before pulling away. His gaze focused intently on her mouth. She beamed at him, and he swallowed before tearing his eyes from her lips. The clearing of a throat behind her made her jump away from him.

Cooper had a smug look on his face as he crossed his arms. June's cheeks heated as she slid into the booth.

"Have you looked at the menu yet?" Her voice trembled in embarrassment. Playing it cool had never been her forte. "I'm thinking tonight calls for something extra greasy and carb laden."

Sosimo glanced around, then sat next to her, though he kept some distance between them. When he pushed his foot up against hers, heat radiated through her. She couldn't help the ridiculous grin that stretched across her face. She moved the menu closer to her face to hide her expression from Cooper across the table.

"Greasy carbs sound good." Sosimo tapped his finger on a bacon cheeseburger with onion rings on his menu, making her stomach growl in response. "I called Zeke to update him on tonight's development."

Cold splashed through her body, replacing the warmth. "Yeah."

"They're gonna look into it."

"That's just it. I've been thinking about it nonstop, and there's no way they should've been able to find us there. Anal doesn't describe how I've been about that place."

"Don't worry, cariña. We'll figure it out." He squeezed her hand.

"You two lovebirds ready to order or what? I'm starving." Cooper waved the waitress over. "Chicken-fried steak with the works, please."

The waitress nodded as she scribbled, then glanced at June.

"I'll have the bacon cheeseburger with onion rings, please." June handed her the menu.

"Can I have the biscuits and gravy with eggs over easy and hash browns?" Sosimo's order made her question her choice.

"Sure thing, hun." The waitress smiled as she grabbed the menus and headed for the kitchen.

June looked up at Sosimo. "I'll trade you an onion ring for a bite or two off your plate."

He brought his hand up to her cheek and softly rubbed under the cut. "You can have whatever you want." He cleared his throat, darted his gaze at Cooper, and dropped his hand. "Does it hurt?"

She shook her head. "It's fine." She lowered her voice though there were few customers there. "What are we going to do?"

"Zeke is calling our friend Lena Rebel to come pick us up. She just retired from the Army, literally landed last week, so no one should be able to connect us." He sighed and squeezed his hands together on the table. "We'll stay at her place tonight."

"Could someone in your company have gone to the dark side?" Cooper asked.

"Maybe, but I keep all my inventions secret until they are under contract. Only then do I bring everyone at the company in."

"So many secrets." Sosimo's voice fell flat.

He didn't know the truth of that statement. She hated them too, the need to watch every word. She wanted to tell him everything, felt the desire building in her chest. She peeked up at him. His cheek flexed as his jaw clenched, causing the words to catch in the back of her mouth. He cleared his throat as the waitress brought their food. She stared at her plate, trying desperately to decide if she should tell him or not.

He bumped her shoulder with his. "We'll figure it out. You don't have to do this alone anymore."

"I don't?" She forced the question through her dry throat.

"No, cariña." He touched the back of her hand. "I'm not leaving you until this is figured out."

Effervescence rushed through her like she'd just chugged three energy drinks. Her body zinged like static electricity as she turned her head to face him, needing to see the truth in his eyes. His gaze held an intensity she'd never witnessed before.

He broke away, glancing at Cooper, then focusing on the table. "Let's eat. Then after a good night's sleep, we can see if we can untangle any of this."

She pulled away and reached her shaking hands for

her burger. The relief of having him here to help overwhelmed her, and she attempted not to cry. She hadn't had help since she started her new life almost ten years ago. Since bawling in her fries wouldn't improve their situation any, she took a bite out of the sandwich. As the saltiness of the bacon and cheese hit her mouth, her body relaxed into the comfort. They would figure this out and get her invention to the right people. Then when they succeeded, she would formulate a plan to keep Sosimo close, no matter the cost.

SOSIMO GLANCED around the dark neighborhood as he followed Reagan into Lena's house. The drive hadn't been long, but Reagan had lain with her head across his legs and fallen asleep almost immediately. The entire ride had him combing his fingers through the tendrils of her hair that refused to stay in her messy bun. Would he be able to keep her safe?

"I only have one spare bedroom." Lena tossed her keys onto the kitchen table.

"No worries. I'll just crash on the floor." Sosimo threaded his fingers through Reagan's as she leaned into his side. "Cooper can have the couch."

"But—"

"No buts, cariña."

"Bossy." She glared at him, though her stifled smile ruined it, and she followed Lena down the hallway.

Sosimo leaned against the back of the couch. If he sat down, he'd probably fall asleep. His eyes scratched with each blink. When was the last time he had been this tired? He couldn't believe they ended up in a city where they knew someone. Being here, he could relax a little more. Or at least try to.

"So you and Reagan?" Cooper stretched onto the couch, a smirk on his face. "That was some pretty intense kissing. Is that why you keep putting me on guard and giving me the night shift? You wanted time to smooch."

"Smooching? Who's been smooching?" Lena came out of the hallway carrying a tote.

"Sosimo and Reagan." Cooper wiggled his eyebrows.

Lena whistled. "Sos, she's hot. You sure you can handle that caliber of woman?"

"Whatever." Sosimo rubbed the back of his neck, then shrugged. "She's amazing. Smartest person I've ever met. I should keep my head on straight, but there's just something about her that makes me want to either whisk her away and hide out forever or take her down to meet mi madre."

"You're in trouble for sure if you want to take her to your family. Your mom would line up the pastor the minute you walked in the door with her." Cooper tsked, crossing his arms under his head.

Sosimo cringed. His mom was still a little bitter about him leaving the church when he found there was more to his faith than just his parents' religion. "She'd want a priest, but wouldn't make too much of a fuss when I refused. At least, I hope she wouldn't."

Sosimo chuckled as warmth spread across his chest. The thought of her doing that didn't have him running for the hills. More like he wondered how soon Reagan could go with him. Yep, he was a goner.

"I recognize her from somewhere." Lena's words pulled him from imagining Reagan in his parents' home.

"¿De veras? Where?"

"That's just it, I can't really place it. I don't think I've met her. Maybe I've seen a picture of her before." She shrugged and slapped the tote she held against Sosimo's stomach. "It'll come to me."

"Well, she invents for the military. Probably a press release or something." Sosimo grabbed onto the tote before it fell to the floor.

"That's probably it." She pointed to the tote. "My brothers insist I keep clothes for them here for those times they swing by. There's probably something the two of you could wear so you could wash your clothes before you leave." She stepped backwards toward the kitchen and waved her hand below her nose. "Hate to break it to you, but you two Joes stink."

Cooper laughed and lunged up from the couch for Lena. "This is manly musk, woman." He cornered her and wrapped her in a bear hug. "You know it attracts you like bees to honey."

"Ugh." Lena quickly darted under Cooper and leaned against the kitchen island. "That may be attractive to you Navy boys, but to those not stuck in a tin can, it's called B.O."

Sosimo laughed. Lena always had been easy to joke with and quick with shooting men down. That was until Ethan Stryker had stolen her heart. Sosimo hadn't seen her since he got out of the Army. Grief still seemed to pull at the corner of her eyes that had always sparkled with joy and grit before. She was a tough one, for sure, not calling it quits when Ethan died in that horrible mission.

Sosimo nodded his head at her across the room. "Thanks for letting us crash here."

"I'm glad I'm able to help."

"What are your plans now that you've retired?"

Lena's shoulders slumped, and she looked away. "Not sure. I moved here when Ethan was still alive, so ..."

"I'm sorry, Lena."

She shrugged. "I'll find something."

"Semper Gumby," Cooper said as he pulled sweats from the tote.

"Man, you know we don't speak Jarhead." Sosimo punched him lightly, and Lena laughed. Sosimo looked at Lena. "You should think about joining us out in Colorado."

"Zeke's been talking to me about it. I've been turning him down, but now—" She rubbed her hands together. "Sounds like it could be fun. Better than hanging out here. Unless Cooper's signed on. I don't think I could hang out with the likes of him for long."

"Hey, I resent that." Cooper pouted. "Besides, Zeke and I have been discussing other plans." He stuck his tongue out. "I'm showering."

Lena rolled her eyes. "Child."

Sosimo rifled through the tote and pulled out a shirt and sweats.

"Go change." Lena motioned toward the hall.

"You've got my room. I'll take the recliner. You need the beauty sleep more than I do."

Sosimo nodded, lifting his hand in thanks as he crossed the room to the hall. He tucked into the bedroom that had the door open and pulled off his shirt. His finger got caught in a hole in the material. What in the world? He smiled as he rushed out and knocked on Reagan's door.

"Come in."

"I forgot to show you something." He shut the door behind him and handed her the shirt.

One of her delicate eyebrows rose as she took the garment. "You want me to look at your filthy shirt?"

He rolled his eyes and ripped it out of her hands. Turning it to the hole, he pointed. "Look. That looks like a bullet hole to me."

Her gasp brought the satisfaction he'd been looking for. Her hand covered her mouth. Man, he could kiss her. She yanked his arm and started twisting him to see the armor suit. He cringed at her rough handling.

He turned so he wouldn't get wrenched around anymore and pointed to where he remembered the impact. "There, cariña."

Her hand rubbed along his back, shooting a trail of sparks across his skin. "It worked."

Her hoarse whisper sent goosebumps where the sparks had been. She'd done it. This would save so many lives if he could just get her to the right people.

He wrapped his arm around her waist and put all his pride and hope into his kiss. He pulled her closer, diving his hands deep into her soft locks she'd let down. He needed to be close to her, to anchor himself to this connection that coursed through his body. She returned his kiss with equal fervor, cupping her delicate hands on his cheeks like she wanted to hold him there. He angled his head so he could claim more of her. He wasn't going anywhere. After what seemed like years and seconds at the same time, their kisses slowed to one long embrace of the lips.

"Ay, caray." Her whisper echoed his feelings exactly, and he smiled against her lips.

He ran a shaky hand down her back. "Boot up your computer. I'll go get out of this so you can analyze it."

She nodded, skimming her hands down his cheeks and behind his ears. "Be quick."

She tugged lightly on his hair, sending another shock wave through him. Her light kiss turned into more until several minutes later he threaded his fingers through hers, still buried deep in his hair. He moved their hands between them and kissed her knuckles.

She huffed, looking thoroughly put off. "Go, but hurry back."

Sosimo rushed to his room and changed into the clothes Lena had given him. He twisted the armor suit in his hands, looking at where the bullet had hit. There wasn't a single mark on it. He crossed the hall to Reagan's room to find her sitting cross-legged on the bed, engrossed in her computer.

"So?" Sosimo tossed the suit on the bed and sat down next to her.

She wrapped her arms around his neck and kissed him

on the cheek. "It's here. It recorded everything, and with the system now communicating flawlessly, soldiers' base command will be able to monitor health while in the field. It's even equipped with a defibrillation system to give the wearer a jolt if their heart rate flatlines." She went back to her computer and pointed at the screen. "This is your heartbeat. What's amazing is that your heart didn't really pick up much until about an hour and a half ago and just a couple minutes before you took it off. Either there's a glitch in the system, or I'm not reading this correctly."

He leaned over and tucked her hair behind her ear. "That's no mistake." He kissed below her ear. "That heart rate increase is all because of you."

She swatted him on the arm and went back to evaluating the data, a blush pinking her neck. "Right here must've been when the bullet impacted." She trailed her finger on the screen. "See how there's a spike on the graph?"

He nodded his head. "That would've been about right. I got hit right after we got out of the house."

She turned to him and started lifting his shirt. "Let me see where it hit."

Sosimo laughed low, glad the suit didn't record his rocketing heartbeat. "For a minute there, I thought I was gonna have to tell you I'm not that kind of guy."

"Good, because I'm not that kind of girl either." She paused and looked into his eyes, her expression urging him to believe the truth of her words.

He kissed her softly on the lips and pulled away. "Is there a bruise?"

"No, nothing. Just the bruise from earlier. What did it feel like when the bullet hit?"

Sosimo skootched back and rested against the head-board. "It felt like someone had punched me in the back. With no one around, I knew it had to be a bullet. But the impact wasn't hard, not something that would throw me off or knock me down. It only alerted me that they had seen us."

She moved next to him, pulling her computer onto her lap and leaning against him. "I'm so glad I had you try that on."

She shivered, and he put his arm around her. He was glad she had too. Otherwise their grand escape would've gone down with him bleeding out in the field after he demanded that Cooper get her out of there.

He closed his eyes and leaned his head against hers. He had to get her to the SEP. This invention would be a game changer for the US military. The tension eased out of his body with the tapping of her fingers on the keyboard. After this crazy road trip finished, he wanted to take her home to meet his madre.

ELEVEN

They were running fast, so fast that June's legs burned.
The forest yanked at them, insidious hands slowing them
down. They broke out of the darkness into the moonlight
of an open field. Goosebumps skittered across her skin
like a million bugs.

"No." She didn't want to go into the telling light.
Didn't want to become exposed.

Sosimo glanced back at her as she pulled on his hand,
slowing him down. "Come on, cariña. We just need to get
to the other side."

She nodded, but her feet weighed a hundred pounds
each. His forehead creased in concern only to widen in
shock. He dropped her hand and touched his chest where
blood ran from an open wound. Another bullet hit,
piercing the armor suit and throwing him backward. She
reached for him as she screamed, but he fell into a gaping
pit. Her fingers skimmed his before he disappeared into
the dark.

June jerked awake, ramming her forehead into her

computer. Pain exploded across her face, bringing tears to her eyes. At least, she thought the pain from smashing her face into the screen, and not the dream, caused the tears. Oh, please let her not be bawling in her sleep.

Sosimo shifted where he'd accidentally fallen asleep next to her while she had analyzed the data. She squeezed her eyes shut and rubbed her head. Not the best way to start a fresh day. She hated when she fell asleep with her computer in bed. It always seemed to end up bad.

The residual fear of the dream caused her to shiver. Warm arms wrapped around her, a chuckle vibrating against her cheek. Would she ever stop making a fool of herself in front of this man? Probably not.

Another knock, not a gunshot, banged on her door. "Hey, man. Zeke wants an update." Cooper's deep voice rumbled through the door.

"All right, I'll be out in a sec." Sosimo pushed her crazy bedhead hair out of her eyes and brushed his thumb across her forehead. "You okay?" He did a poor job at hiding the laughter in his voice.

"Hazards of falling asleep while working."

He kissed her on the forehead and got off the bed. She couldn't believe they had both fallen asleep. She waited for the embarrassment to come, but only the effects of a well-rested night remained.

"Come out when you're ready. We need to figure out what we do next." Sosimo backed toward the door.

She nodded absentmindedly as she glanced around the room. Her brain still tried to recover from the nightmare.

Sosimo smiled widely. "You're adorable when you're confused. I could get used to seeing this side of you every morning."

Before she could reply, he vanished out the door. Her heart pounded violently in her chest. Had he just said what she thought he did? She went over his words again in her head. She nodded unconsciously as hope and warmth invaded her chest. She forced the feeling down. He hadn't declared his love or anything.

She focused on rereading her notes from the night before. Excitement built again, energizing her more than coffee ever had. She scrambled off the bed and rushed out of the bedroom with her computer.

"Sosimo, you've got to—" June's words stalled in her throat as Sosimo gave her a halting motion with his hand from the kitchen island stools.

Lena pushed something around in the skillet on the stove. Cooper popped bread into the toaster. The smell should have had her stomach protesting for a bite, but the tension in Sosimo's shoulders turned her stomach in somersaults. Looked like breakfast was out of the question.

"Miss MacArthur, I'm glad you've joined us." Zeke's voice came over the phone's speaker.

"I thought we agreed to call me Reagan?" She crossed to the kitchen and leaned against the counter.

"Sorry." Zeke didn't sound sorry. He sounded ... guarded. "This plan isn't working."

June's heart dropped into her stomach as her gaze shot to Sosimo just in time to see his jaw clench. "I beg your pardon, sir, but Sosimo and Cooper have been doing an amazing job."

"I thought we agreed to call me Zeke?" His tone had lightened.

"Touché."

June pointed at Cooper's coffee mug and pointed to herself. She would need that coffee after all. Cooper gave her a thumbs up, opened the cabinet, and pulled out a clean mug.

"I'm not questioning my men's abilities to keep you safe. Far from. But when a plan isn't working, you adjust and recalculate." Zeke's tone reminded her of her father's at the moment, all fall-in-line soldier. She hated that tone.

"But—"

"It's necessary, Reagan." Sosimo grabbed the mug of coffee from Cooper and handed it to her. "These guys seem to know our every move."

June wrapped her hands around the lifeline the mug provided. She didn't know what upset her most, that she felt out of control or the fact that both Zeke and Sosimo reminded her so much of her father. She pushed the disappointment to the depth of her stomach like she had her entire life.

"So, what's the plan?" June took a fortifying drink of the hot coffee.

"We were just getting ready to discuss that." Sosimo scooped his spoon in his bowl of cereal and took a big bite, making her stomach growl.

"We hoped that we could get some information off of the men that ambushed us in Aspen." Zeke sighed. "Rafe ran their prints and facial recognition through all the databases and came up empty everywhere."

Cooper whistled low. June's heart dropped to her feet. She understood how hard it was to hide identities so thoroughly. Hadn't she done that for herself? She peeked at Sosimo before looking into the bracing liquid steaming from her mug. She needed to tell him about herself, the guilt of not yet doing so weighed heavily on her, but his reaction to her secret about the invention kept the truth bottled up inside. Would he understand her need for privacy, or would he only see the lie she told? The coffee soured in her belly, and she swallowed down the acid that rose up her throat.

"Everywhere Rafe digs we keep coming up against a wall. Whoever these guys are, they're extremely well-funded." A tapping noise came through the phone. "The only thing we can think of is that somehow it's connected to your contact at the SEP."

"No way." June stood up straight, shaking her head at the audacity. She slammed her mug on the counter. "Adam would never be behind something like this."

"It might not be your friend, but it could be someone linked to him through the program." Sosimo touched her elbow. "We just need to be cautious in how we proceed."

She narrowed her eyes at him as implications swirled in her brain. "So what are you suggesting?"

"You can't go to the Soldier Enhancement Program just yet. Not until we have more time to investigate." Zeke's command came through the phone with ultimate authority.

June attempted to think rationally about the situation, but frustration hampered her thoughts. The reason she'd set up the business the way she had and left her old identity behind was so she could make her own decisions. Now, here she sat, stuck in a tangle of lies and trouble with no control of what happened next.

"So, what? We just hang out here?" June flinched at the attitude in her voice. Her sass would horrify her father.

"No, we'll keep heading east, lying as low as we can. We want you as close to the SEP as possible, so when we figure this mess out, you can get your invention to the right people." Sosimo scooped another bite from his cereal, and she had the infantile urge to smack the spoon from his hand.

She crossed her arms with a nod. "Ok. I need to contact my father."

"Is that necessary?" The spoon stopped halfway to Sosimo's mouth.

"Do you want the cavalry sent out after me when I don't?"

His eyelids closed to slits as he surveyed her. Cooper cocked his eyebrow at her from across the kitchen, and Lena paused in scooping the food to a plate. Shoot. June had probably said too much. She needed to beat a fast retreat before she blew everything.

"That's fine. Just make it quick and give out no information." Zeke's agreement came gruff and low through the phone.

She stifled a salute as she turned on her heel and marched to her room. Pride surged through her when she closed the door with a soft click. Plopping on the side of the bed, she rested her head in her hands.

She'd created Reagan so she could make her own decisions and get out from under her father's command. What a web of deception she found herself tangled in. The image of Sosimo's shirt stained red with blood hit her just as sharply as it had in her dream. All indignation drained from her into the plush carpet.

Sosimo and his friends were only trying to keep her safe. The men behind the attacks were the ones stripping her of her freedoms and jeopardizing the lives of good people. She needed to keep her sense of injustice firmly focused on the right source.

She sighed. She owed Sosimo and the others an apology, but first, she had a call to make. She reached for the phone. She just hoped she would be the one to tell the general she had blown up her house. Otherwise, more than just binary rifle targets and propane would be exploding.

SOSIMO FINISHED HIS CEREAL, washed his bowl, and grabbed another cup of coffee and an apple for Reagan, all without showing his raging guilt for running ramrod over her. He'd pissed her off if the stiff shoulders and icy glare told him anything. He had enough sisters to know it did. What surprised him was the lack of a slamming door. Growing up, that sound had always followed his sisters' tantrums.

Not that Reagan had thrown one. He understood her

anger over the invasion of her life. He just hoped she'd realize the need to lie low for a bit longer.

He tried to push aside the unease the rest of the phone call had caused after Reagan had stomped off. Rafe still hadn't been able to find information on her either. He complained that her past was too squeaky clean, too perfect. That she had to be hiding something, because no one could be that good.

Sosimo shook his head. If anyone could come through life without a lot of mars, it would be the homeschooled science geek that jumped from base to base. He shook off the tightness in his chest Rafe's suggestions created and raised his hand to knock, only to pause at the sound of her voice.

"No, Dad, you aren't listening, again." Her huff traveled through the door. "I blew up my house. Me."

Sosimo's mouth dropped open. Why in the world had she told her father that?

"It was the only way to get us an opening to escape." She paused, and Sosimo held his breath. "I'm fine. Sosimo got us out of there without a problem."

He wondered why she'd tell her dad about blowing up the house but leave out the part about her invention working. Guess she didn't want her father worrying too much.

"Yes, I know. You told me they were the best, and you weren't lying. Sosimo is amazing." While her declaration set heat racing through his veins, he wondered how her father knew them.

"Ugh, Dad, there's no tone in my voice. I'm agreeing with you." Her footsteps went one way, then paced the other. "I know, I know. The Army produces men and women of extreme caliber, able to adapt and conquer any situation." She spoke with the tone of someone rolling their eyes at an oft repeated phrase.

The phrase wiggled something in his memory. He couldn't place it, but he had heard those exact words before. He shook off the memory and knocked.

"Listen, Dad. I have to go." Her voice grew closer, and he took a step back. "Yes, I'll call. I love you."

She opened the door, her smile briefly spreading across her face when she glanced in his hand. She grabbed the mug and averted her gaze. Her bag sat on her bed with her stuff spread out around it.

"Thanks." She sat on the edge of the bed. "Listen, I owe you guys an apology. I shouldn't have gotten snarky with you. You're just trying to keep me safe."

"Trust me, you weren't." Sosimo tossed the apple in the air and plopped down next to her. "It can't be easy having life in chaos like it is. I'm sorry we can't just take your invention there without worrying that it's going to still end up in the wrong hands."

She took a drink of the coffee, licked her lips, shrugged. Leaning over, she gently kissed him. "Thanks for being so sweet."

A soft knock sounded on the door followed by Cooper's voice. "Guys, we should probably get on the move."

Sosimo rolled his eyes and smiled at Reagan. "Yes, Mom, we'll be right there."

"Whatever, dude." Cooper huffed through the door. "We're leaving in five, so finish up your make-out session so we can get a move on."

Reagan hid her laugh behind her hands, her face turning bright red. He leaned forward and kissed her on the cheek before heading toward the door. He looked back to find her watching him, so he winked. She might be hiding something, but he knew the heart of her. Whatever the truth was, it couldn't be that bad.

TWELVE

June typed in the backseat of the SUV they had bought in Kentucky, poring over her data and compiling it into an updated report for the SEP. She shifted in her seat, her stuff strewn across the back seat. She missed their RV. Maybe she and Sosimo could get another one and go on a different road trip. One that didn't involve a death race and assassins.

The sun had faded into night, and the lights of whatever city they were in now twinkled like stars on her computer screen. The city street was lined with restaurants and businesses, making her hope they stopped somewhere they could eat. She rubbed her eyes and closed the computer. She wanted to crash. How could driving be so exhausting? All she'd done was sit all day.

Reaching into her backpack, she pulled out the box of Lemonheads Sosimo had bought her at the last stop. He'd been doing that all day, finding little ways to do something special for her. A slow grin built, and she fiddled with her collar as she remembered the kiss he'd given her a few hours back. They'd stopped at a park to stretch their legs. She could still feel the rough bark of the tree he'd pressed her against as he'd kissed the living daylights out of her. He'd had all this pent-up energy, like he'd been waiting for a moment all day to do that.

She glanced up and caught his gaze in the rearview mirror. His tempting lips cocked in a knowing one-sided smile, and his eyes teased her. She rolled her eyes and gazed out the window, hoping the interior of the car hid her blush. If the heat of the thing had any correlation to the color, her face rivaled Ronald McDonald's hair.

"Let's see if they have a room here." Sosimo pulled up to a hotel's door, and jumped out.

"So, Cooper, something I've been wondering about. If you were a part of the Marines, how do you know Sosimo and the rest of Zeke's gang?" June had loved listening to their stories all day as they volleyed back and forth, but all the stories had been more a competition between Army and Marines which had left her confused.

He turned in the seat and smiled back at her. He had a quiet nature that resembled her own, but when he talked, she felt as if she were visiting with an old friend. She wished she'd learned that kind of social fluidity.

"I was a raider with the Special Operations Command. Before that I was a sniper. We worked jointly on several missions and were camped at the same bases the last few years." Cooper shrugged, a casual gesture, but June knew the caliber of men accepted into the MARSOC.

Her father tried to pull them in on as many missions as he could. When the division had been created, her father had said it was about time the Marines got with the program. Then again, her father was more than a little biased.

"Of course, all that was before South America." He shook his head, his voice emerging raspy. "It was a shame when Zeke's crew had that mission go south. We lost Ethan Stryker, then their captain disappeared in the Colorado mountains. After that, one-by-one, they all got out when it was time to reenlist. I don't blame them. None of them came back from that mission whole."

She wrapped her arms around her even though the vehicle's heater ran. "Is that where Jake lost his leg?"

"Yeah. Sosimo blames himself, but Zeke says that's not how it went down." Cooper rubbed the back of his neck. "It's funny the lies we allow ourselves to believe. Every single one of us have ghosts of past missions that haunt us." His southern accent, that he'd hidden, thickened as his emotion increased.

"That's what drives me. Those ghosts." June looked at her bag like she could see through the fabric to the computer within. "I saw so many of them hovering above the soldiers at the base and haunting the injured in the military hospital I volunteered at in Germany. I want to do whatever I can to make it safer." She huffed, swallowing the emotion that clogged her throat, and looked up at him. "I know that sounds ridiculous. Men and women join the military knowing they could be put in danger. Yet, if something I invent lessens that, even a little, and gives our soldiers protection, I'll give anything to make that happen."

He held her gaze for a span of several seconds, then

nodded. "I know why Sosimo loves you. You're quite the force to be reckoned with."

"Sosimo doesn't lov—"

"Please, the man has fallen hard." Cooper turned forward and collected his gear. "You don't talk about taking a girl home to your parents, especially not Madre Rivas, and not mean business."

Life slowed as her brain computed what he said. A tingling started at the top of her head and rushed through her body. Sosimo climbed into the vehicle. She stared at him, her mouth gaping open unattractively. Could this amazing man love her? She knew he liked her, but love? It was too good to hope for.

He glanced between her and Cooper, tilting his head to one side. "What?"

"Nothing, man. Just telling embarrassing stories of you, that's all." Cooper turned around and winked.

Sosimo groaned as he put the vehicle in drive and pulled into a parking spot. "I knew I couldn't trust you to behave."

Cooper chuckled, pushing the door open. "Nope. Where's the fun in behaving?"

June flinched as the door slammed shut, jarring her out of her stupor. Sosimo loved her? He opened her door and reached his hand in to help her out. Skin slid upon skin, shooting buzzing jolts straight up her arm. He might not love her; she wouldn't know until he confirmed the allegation. She most certainly loved him. So now what?

As she climbed out of the vehicle, one thing became evident. She didn't want to hide from this. She had done enough of that over the last ten years to make her sick. As dangerous as confessing it might be, she couldn't veil her feelings anymore.

She stepped up to him, fisting his shirt in her hands and pushing him against the car door. His eyebrows rose the second before she pressed her lips against his. Everything faded to nothing except him and his arms circling around her. Traffic disappeared until she only heard the dancing of their breath as he pulled her tighter to him. How could the world stop yet spin wildly at the same time? This man defied physics.

She pulled back just a hair, a tightness in her gut. "I love you." Her whispered confession broke the bubble of silence and rushed the sound of traffic to her ears.

He stared into her eyes and swallowed. The silence that now stretched between them sucked her confidence like a black hole. She stepped back, only to have him tighten his grip.

"No, I need to be right here in this amazing moment a little longer." He buried his face into her neck, his inhale skating across the skin and diving into her heart. He pressed his lips below her ear, and her knees turned to jelly. "I love you too, cariña."

If the joy that filled her heart could burst out in light, she'd shine as bright as the sun. Bubbly laughter bounced out of her as she threw her arms around his neck and kissed him again. His lips smiled against hers. The feel of the upturned shape settled her nerves.

"Could we please go up to the room now?" Cooper's voice sounded from the bumper of the SUV. "I promise I won't gag in my mouth too much if you want to make moon-eyes at each other."

Sosimo chuckled as he ran his hand down her cheek. "We should go inside where it's safe."

She nodded and grabbed her backpack. When they got to the room door, Sosimo let go of her hand and motioned for her to stay while he searched the room. She stared blankly into space, a giddy smile stretched across her lips.

Cooper bumped her in the back. "Told you."

"Shh." She threw a glare behind her as Sosimo's, "Clear," sounded from the room.

"Did you see the Cracker Barrel next door?" June threw herself across the far bed, her arm draped over her eyes. "We are definitely stopping there before we head wherever it is we're going tomorrow. Their country fried steak breakfast is amazing."

"How can you even think about food right now?" Cooper's shocked tone had her lifting her arm to look at him. He rubbed his gut, a pained look on his face. "I don't even want to think about food after that barbecue, and you ate almost as much as me."

Sosimo tossed his bag onto the desk, then peeked out the window before pulling the curtains closed. "She's either starving herself or gorging. There doesn't seem to be an in-between."

"It's all these nerves." June rose and pushed herself against the headboard. "I think I might comfort myself through my stomach." She pointed at Cooper. "You want to do me a favor?"

"No, I won't go get ice so you two can make out more." He crossed his arms.

Her ears heated. Great. No darkness to hide her

blush now. "No, I'm wondering if you could try on my suit? I want to make sure the programming works with a different operator. That nothing glitches in the biometrics."

Cooper froze, his eyes not blinking from his look of awe. "You want me to try on the Supersuit?"

June threw her head back and laughed. "It's just an armored suit, nothing super about it."

"That's not true. It's the most amazing invention I've ever seen." Sosimo plopped onto the edge of the bed, placing her legs over his lap.

"It won't fit me." Cooper motioned up and down his body. "My superior physique won't fit in anything puny Sosimo's did."

June looked at Sosimo, her nose scrunching as she thought. "There's nothing puny about Sosimo."

"Gracias, amor." He leaned forward and kissed her quickly.

She smiled before turning to Cooper. "Besides, I designed the suit to adjust to whoever wore it."

"There's no way you can wear something I can." Cooper snatched the suit she tossed to him and examined it.

She smirked. "I bet you the treat of your choice it will. You try it on, let me run some tests. Then, I'll try it on."

He rolled his shoulders and met her gaze. "I'll take that bet." He sauntered into the bathroom.

"Coop, make sure you pull your pants on over the suit. Reagan has delicate sensibilities," Sosimo hollered and leaned sideways, his voice pitching low as he slid his hand up her arm. "I have to say, I'm looking forward to seeing you in that suit."

He cupped his hand around the back of her neck and pulled her to him. Her fingers ached as she wrapped her hand around his arm to steady herself. His bicep flexed. Definitely nothing puny about him. He hovered above her lips, closing his eyes and inhaling deeply. Then, with great tenderness, he kissed her.

"Mmm, lemons." He dove in for another taste.

The door to the bathroom opened, and she jumped away from him. He raised his eyebrow as he tapped her leg. Oh, he knew perfectly well what he put her through.

She cleared her throat and surveyed Cooper, who strutted out and struck a pose. He then grew serious as he moved and stretched in the suit. It fit him as perfectly as it had Sosimo. She swung her legs off the bed and crossed to examine it closer.

"How does it feel?" She moved his arms up and peered at the seams. "Any pinching?"

"It feels great." He rotated his shoulders. "I'm not sure I've ever worn something so comfortable before. This can't be strong enough to protect you from bullets."

She clicked the suit on and went to her computer. She booted up the program and smiled when Cooper's heartbeat played through the speakers. She closed her eyes and bit her lip to keep from beaming.

"It works, chamo." Sosimo's quick defense added to her sense of happiness. "Remember, I was shot in the back, would've killed me. I barely felt it. She's designed it to somehow distribute the force of the impact."

"Cool." Cooper smoothed his hand down the front of him. "This will change everything."

A silence settled over them as everyone paused. Her eyes stung as she inhaled, the weight of what this invention could do settling over her. She should've worked faster. Should've put more time in. Hadn't she been working on it for years? What if she could've saved their friend? A tear rushed down her cheek, and Sosimo caught it.

"Cariña?"

"I'm so sorry." She sniffed, trying desperately to stop the tears that threatened. "I should've made this a priority. Should've put in longer hours. How many lives could it have saved if I would've just tried harder to figure it out?"

"No, Reagan, don't think like that." Sosimo scooted to her and pulled her close. "You've done so much for soldiers both on and off the field. Never think you haven't. Look at all you've done through *A Hero's Tomorrow*."

"But how many of them wouldn't need prosthetics if I'd just gotten this done earlier? Jake was shot. If he would've had a suit on, he wouldn't have lost his leg."

He forced her to look at him. "You are only one person, and you've helped incredibly. Now, with this, you'll help even more. Don't put that on you, amor. That's a weight you can't carry."

"Yeah, Reagan." Cooper rolled his shoulders. "We're vanquishing ghosts today, not taking more on."

The truth of their comments settled over her, suffocating the self-doubt and giving comfort. Their words held a truth she needed to accept. Her next breath came a little easier as she let go. She may not be able to work faster, but she'd keep inventing, doing her part for those who protected their freedom.

Sosimo rubbed his thumb over her cheek. "Better?" He smiled when she nodded. "Good. Because I'm ready to see what you look like in that thing."

She laughed as Cooper tucked into the bathroom to change out of it. How could she have ended up so blessed? Not only did these guys protect her from danger, but they protected her from herself. She had lived in self-doubt for so long, always questioning if she'd done the right thing, that it felt good to be dragged from that smothering pit.

She peered at Sosimo where he dug through his gear. Yes, she'd been blessed beyond belief. Now, she needed to find the courage to reveal her identity. She just didn't want to broach that while they were still thick in this situation. She couldn't handle the stress of running for her life and the fallout of Sosimo's rejection if he decided he couldn't take her lies.

THIRTEEN

Sosimo's body sagged in relief as he peered across the river two mornings later. They'd made it to Virginia. They'd rented a little two-bedroom waterfront cottage north of Fort Belvoir and eaten a magnificent seafood dinner, much to Reagan's delight. Before they turned in for the night, he'd sat on the dock with Reagan watching the birds and water rush by.

They'd talked for hours, though they both were exhausted. He'd never found someone outside his men and family he could be at ease with as much as he was with her. When all of this was done, maybe they could come back here, spend some time exploring the coast and sitting on the dock long after the stars came out. Maybe it'd take a while before they could get her before the SEP. Wouldn't that be a blessing in disguise?

When they'd finally gone to bed, he'd slept horribly, despite the comfy couch. Maybe the night before they'd gotten to Virginia had spoiled him. He smiled remembering that night in the hotel room. She had refused to allow him to sleep on the floor, claiming she'd plop down next to him if he wanted to be so silly. So Reagan had nestled under the covers and him on top of them. When he'd woken up, she had her hand wrapped around his arm, and the rising sun had made her look ethereal as it haloed her head. Last night, he'd felt lost without her close and had tossed and turned all night.

Soft footsteps sounded over the lapping water. He turned to see Reagan wrapped in a blanket, clutching a mug of coffee in her hands. Her hair still flew wildly about her head, and the rising sun made the ginger strands shine copper.

"Wow, how beautiful." She peered across the water pinked with the sunrise.

He stared at her and swallowed the lump in his throat. "Precioso."

She peeked at him, and her smile grew. "You aren't even looking."

"Why would I waste my time with that, when I have you to look at?" He stepped closer, and his voice came out low and husky. "Did you sleep well?"

She shivered, her eyes closing as he ran his hand through her hair. "No."

"Why not?" He eased his fingers across her shoulders.

She shrugged and took a drink of her steaming coffee. A blush crept up her neck. Or was that just the pink from the sun?

"Cariño, you weren't worrying over stuff you can't change again, were you?"

"No." She shook her head and handed him her mug. "It's silly ... but I missed you."

Her words warmed his insides more than the hot coffee. He set the mug on the dock's railing. Stepping closer, he kissed her slowly, pulling her tighter when she sighed in contentment.

"I missed you, too."

Her phone trumpeted the *Reveille* in her sweatshirt pocket, vibrating between them. He hadn't heard that since he'd left the Army and almost snapped to attention. She cringed and stepped away from him.

Putting the phone to her ear, she turned toward the house. "Dad, you realize it's still too early to be calling?"

Sosimo grabbed the mug and took another drink.

"No, Dad. It's not necessary. We're safe where we are." Her shoulders slumped, and defeat laced her voice.

Sosimo stepped up next to her. She clenched her free hand into the blanket, making her look small and vulnerable. He leaned on the railing, hoping his relaxed posture calmed her.

"Junebug, it's not a request." The harsh command was loud enough that Sosimo could hear and had him squeezing the mug so he wouldn't take the phone from her hands and do something stupid, like chew out his hopefully future father-in-law or chuck the phone into the Potomac.

"I'm not one of your grunts you can order around, General." Her retort both impressed and worried him.

What did she mean, general? Sosimo turned around, placing his back to the railing, and peered back at her.

Her chin trembled before she tipped her head back and stared at the sky as the voice spoke rapidly at her.

"Fine. We'll be there later this morning," she agreed without emotion.

Her father barked something else.

"Don't push it, Dad. I said we'd be there later this morning." At least some of her spunk had returned as she sharply tapped the end call icon and shoved the phone in her pocket.

Her eyes quickly darted to Sosimo before she leaned over the railing with a sigh. "My father wants us to go to Fort Meade where he's stationed. He thinks we'll be safer there. He's not willing to wait any longer and plans on throwing his resources at this to help."

He rubbed his hand across her shoulders, but she didn't lean into him. She straightened and angled her body away from him. Something about going to her parents had her guard up.

"I'm going to go get ready." She looked back over the river, her eyes filled with so much sorrow that Sosimo wanted to pull her in tight and whisk her away from all of this.

"Okay." He cleared his throat that had gone dry.

She nodded and turned toward the cottage. Her steps plodded heavily on the wooden dock. Something about this entire situation gave Sosimo an empty feeling in his gut, like dread pooled there, hungrily devouring all the hope from the last few days. Why would she pull away from him like she had? Was Rafe right about her hiding something? What an idiot. Hadn't he known she hid something from the beginning? He just hoped the truth didn't blow their relationship to smithereens. He pulled out his phone.

"You realize it's four in the morning, right?" Rafe's annoyed voice rasped through the phone. "How's a man supposed to get his beauty sleep if his so-called friends keep waking him up?"

"Listen, Reagan's father called. Ordered us to go to Fort Meade where he's stationed." Sosimo rubbed the back of his neck. "I feel like I'm flying blind here."

"Did you ask her who her pops is?" Rustling sounded through the phone.

Sosimo tossed the coffee into the river, his gut twisting. He hadn't asked her. Kept hoping she'd tell him, but with each passing moment that she didn't, the doubt crept in.

"I'll take your silence as a no." Rafe huffed. "What's going on, man?"

"I think I did something stupid."

After a pause, Rafe growled. "Okay, what?"

"Ay caraye, I fell in love with her."

"Hot dog, now we're talking." Rafe's voice held an excitement that made Sosimo cringe. "She's smoking."

"Rafe." Sosimo put as much menace as he could in his voice.

"Calm down. Though, I could've called it from that first night at the fundraiser." Rafe's voice turned dramatic. "Something about the way you glared at her screamed wedding bells as you escorted her around the ballroom."

"Yeah, well, those bells may come crashing down."

Sosimo spun the mug on his finger. "Just see what you can find, okay?"

"On it."

The phone went dead. Sosimo stared at it in his hand. Why was he so hesitant to ask her? Was he worried she'd lie? Or was he more scared she'd tell the truth? He stomped to the cottage. Whether she told him or not, he'd have answers to at least part of the mystery in a matter of hours. He prayed the truth didn't rip his heart out in the discovering.

JUNE CLENCHED her hands around the steering wheel as the soldier at the guardhouse took one look at her and waved them in. Sosimo gazed at her. The question he'd never asked and she'd been too chicken to answer zinged across the space between them. She'd hopped in the driver's seat after they'd eaten breakfast, needing the East Coast traffic to distract her. But the closer they got to the fort, the thicker the tension became.

Now her silence had built a wall of steel between them, blocking the friendship and love that had flowed so freely. Stupid cowardice. She should've just told him.

Her stomach twisted, and she was glad she'd just pushed her eggs around her plate without eating them. She pulled onto her parents' road where the nicer houses sat in the fort. Cooper cleared his throat, his eyes meeting hers in the rearview mirror. She pulled into her parents' drive and swallowed the bile that rose up her throat.

"June Paxton," Cooper whispered in the back, causing Sosimo to twist in his seat to look back at him.

She put the car in park and turned off the ignition, a sense of finality settling with the dying engine. She bit her lip and glanced at Sosimo. His eyes had trained on the front door that opened to General Daniel Paxton, her father, marching out. Sosimo's eyes narrowed and his jaw clenched as he stared at her father getting closer. Sosimo's eyes didn't avert to her once.

Her heart sank as she reached for the door. "I'm sorry. I should've—"

"Yeah. You should've." Sosimo yanked open his door and exited, approaching Dad with a salute.

She closed her eyes, knocking her head against the headrest before pushing the door open.

Cooper came up next to her. "Don't worry. He'll get over it."

"I doubt it." She didn't look at him, just grabbed her bag from the backseat.

"Junebug." Dad eased her bag off her shoulder as he wrapped an arm around her.

"Dad." She leaned into his embrace. No matter how much she didn't like her father's intrusion, his presence comforted her.

"Let's go inside. Your mom just finished baking your favorite banana bread." He ushered everyone in, pointing to the corner of the entryway. "Drop your gear right there and follow me."

June rolled her eyes as she followed him down the hall to the kitchen. General Paxton led in full command mode. She crossed to her mom and gave her a kiss on the cheek. Where her father was all hard with his lean, muscular body and his short military-issue haircut, her mother had soft curves and a short blonde bob that had lightened to white. The smell of baked bananas and cinnamon filled the kitchen, soothing June's frazzled nerves down a notch or two.

"June, I'm so glad you're here." Hearing her real name from her mother's lips startled her.

When had she ceased being plain ol' June? Should it worry her that her old name itched and felt binding around her? She'd never wanted to leave June completely behind, but somewhere along the way she had.

Dad pointed to the stools lining the counter. "Have a seat, men. My Claire's made her famous banana bread. You won't taste any better than this."

"Oh, stop, Danny. You're embarrassing me." Mom blushed, swatting at her father's arm.

June's gaze bounced between her parents. When had they gotten so flirty? Her eyes widened a fraction before she ducked her head and reached for a plate. She couldn't remember a time when they'd shown such love toward each other. Definitely not since her brother's death. She blinked as she grabbed a piece of bread.

"I just want to say that I appreciate how you've kept my Junebug safe." Her father pointed his coffee mug at Sosimo and Cooper before taking a drink.

"Dad, really?" She hated feeling like a teenager again, just waiting for the next embarrassing thing her father would say.

"We take our job seriously, sir." Sosimo's expression was all business, a soldier at attention.

"I knew you boys were the best." Dad nodded with a tsk. "Wish you all hadn't gotten out. Your team was one of the best we've ever had."

"Thank you, sir." Sosimo fidgeted on his stool and swallowed.

"I've contacted Adam. He'll be here shortly to pick up your contraption." Her father's audacity had her gaping at him.

"But, Dad—"

"June, it's past time for you to pass that project on and move on to the next one. It won't do anyone any good if it never makes it to our troops." Dad took a swig of his coffee. "Your last little gadget has been a big help in the field. I can only imagine that this will be the same."

"Sir, do you know what she's been working on?" Sosimo sat up straighter and turned to her. "You told him what you are working on, right?"

The accusation stung. "Of course I did." She bit out, crossing her arms as the freezing reality of her own false-hood bloomed in her chest. "Kind of."

Sosimo snorted, shaking his head before he turned to her father. "Sir, her project is an armored suit that not only absorbs the impact somehow but also monitors the wearer's biometrics and can defibrillate the wearer's heart if needed. A shot hit me in the back as we fled her house. Felt like I was hit by a rainbow just starting basic. Didn't even leave a bruise."

Her father's eyes pivoted to her. Nuts. Another truth she'd omitted. She ducked her head and took a bite of bread even though it tasted like sawdust.

"June, you didn't tell me they shot at you."

"Gracious Lord above." Mom fanned herself with her towel.

June swallowed, hoping the bite didn't stick in her throat, and steeled her shoulders. "It wasn't necessary for you to know. We took care of the situation. There wasn't any reason to worry you."

"June." Her mother tsked.

"Not any reason to—"

"Did you not hear what he said?" she interrupted her father, pointing at Sosimo.

He and Cooper flinched and busied themselves with their refreshments. She doubted anyone had ever dared cut off the general. She wasn't one of his soldiers, though he treated her like one.

"My invention will save countless lives, Dad. Not just save them but make it so they can continue to fight those attacking." She paced the length of the kitchen. "People aren't after me for my good looks or my money or even my connection to you. They somehow found out about my invention and want to turn the tables in their direction."

"It's why we've refrained from contacting Adam and the SEP, sir. We think there might be a connection to the terrorists at the program." Sosimo took the last bite of his bread and smiled at June's mom. "That was delicious, Mrs. Paxton. Thank you."

June rolled her eyes as her mother beamed broadly. "Why, thank you, young man."

"We'll sort this out now that you're here. As soon as Adam arrives, we can get people on this." Dad crossed his arms like he'd solved everything.

"I sure hope we can, sir. We've had our best man on this, and he hasn't been able to find a thing." Sosimo's voice echoed her doubt.

"Rafe Malone?" Dad's eyebrows winged up when Sosimo nodded, only to return to his normal scowl. "Hmm. We'll figure this out." His normal commander confidence was firmly in place. "Claire, hun, why don't you show these boys to the spare rooms."

"Follow me, gentlemen. Danny, darling, don't exasperate our daughter while I'm gone." Mom motioned, and the guys fell in line like dutiful soldiers, leaving June to fend for herself.

With the sound of their retreating steps growing smaller, Dad cleared his throat. "It seems you haven't been forthright, June. And from the expression on that young man's face, it hasn't been with just me."

She broke her piece of bread into pieces on her plate. How could she respond when he spoke the absolute truth? Her life had become so full of half-truths and secrets.

"I told you when you came up with this whole Reagan idea that I didn't want you losing yourself in the process of distancing from me." Her father's scolding continued to chip at her bruised heart. "The June I know and love would never keep information from those she loves or put others in danger over her own pride. I'll go debrief with your security team." He headed out of the kitchen, speaking over his shoulder as he went. "I'm not sure if I could trust what you say right now."

June slumped on the stool. Had she really let the betrayal of one man cause the distrust of all? She thought back to her tight-lipped policy and rigid contracts her few employees had to sign. She'd even invented an elaborate manufacturing warehouse so they could create her inventions with the least amount of humans possible. All so she could keep her ideas safe, supposedly out of the hands of the enemy. Had she gone too far?

She glanced up at the ceiling where the heavy footsteps of men sounded. Hopefully her lies hadn't pushed the only man who had ever understood her away. She shuddered and stabbed the crumbs on her plate at the possibility of never seeing Sosimo again.

FOURTEEN

Sosimo leaned against the mantel as Reagan's—scratch that, June Paxton's—friend and contact at the SEP, Adam Johnson, came through the front door. Decorated colonel and long-time friend of the general's, Sosimo remembered a few missions under the man's command. The last mission he'd ever had in the Army was under Colonel Johnson's direction. Though the last mission had gone horribly wrong, the other missions had been solid, some of the best-planned ones they'd had. As much as he hated to admit it, it'd be good to have more resources to sort this trouble out.

He tried not to let his eyes follow Reagan ... June as she hugged Colonel Johnson and motioned for him to take a seat. Sosimo failed, miserably. All color had left her face, making freckles pop out along her nose that weren't normally so apparent. She'd hardly talked the hour they waited, only interjecting information during the debrief when necessary. All the fire had burned out of her.

He vacillated between wanting to wrap her in his

arms and promising they'd figure this all out, to wishing he could leave that second and never see her again. How could she have kept something as big as her identity from him?

When he'd called Rafe to tell him to focus all his energy on the terrorists since they had solved the mystery of Reagan's identity, all the guys had erupted into disbelieving chaos. He really hated speaker phone mode. Wished he could've just told Rafe, hung up, then not heard the shock and, worse, the apologies. He'd have to remind Rafe that he didn't have to blab everything everyone told him. Some things could be left unsaid.

Reagan followed Colonel Johnson to the couch. Her gaze briefly bounced to Sosimo's, only to have her duck away like a scared mouse. His heart ripped even more in his chest. Reagan wasn't a mouse. She was vibrance and compassion, brightness shining in the dark. Sure, she might be awkward and not know exactly what to say in every situation, but that was what pulled him to her, a combination unlike any he'd ever seen before.

He shook the thought away. What did it matter anyway? She'd lied to him. He didn't care what kind of animal she now resembled.

Now who was lying?

General Paxton settled into his armchair with a serious expression on his face. "It's good to see you, Adam. It's been way too long."

"You too, Dan. How is it we're less than two hours away, yet we hardly ever have time to go golfing?" The colonel relaxed into the corner of the couch, crossing his leg over his opposite knee.

"How's your granddaughter doing?"

"Lily's not doing well at all, actually." Colonel Johnson swallowed.

"What's wrong with Lily?" Reagan placed a hand on his arm, her head tilting to one side.

"She was diagnosed with ovarian cancer a year ago."

"But she's still in high school." Reagan put her hand over her mouth.

"We've helped her parents however we can, but the diagnosis isn't looking good." Colonel Johnson picked at the seam of the couch arm as silence settled over the room.

"Adam, please let me know if there is anything that I can do to help." Reagan twisted her hands in her lap. That compassion Sosimo loved so much emerged. He glanced out the front window to keep from moving to the couch to comfort her.

Johnson nodded, a look flitting across his face that Sosimo couldn't place, and cleared his throat. "So, June, did you get all the kinks out of the suit?"

"Yeah, it seems to run exactly like I designed." Her voice had lost all of its emotion again.

"I can tell you, the board members of the SEP have really been eager to see this suit of yours in action." Johnson's enthusiasm rang false in Sosimo's ears.

The hair on the back of his neck rose. He shifted, narrowing his eyes at Johnson. Something had changed since the last time he'd been under his command. A bead of sweat ran down the normally confident man's face. Sosimo shook down the unease.

"Can I see it?" The man's eager tone brought it back up.

Johnson took the suit from Reagan's hand and twisted it in all directions. "I finally get to see it." He smiled at her, before turning his attention back to the suit. "I'm glad you made it here safe. After the incident at your house, I was worried you wouldn't make it here."

"My house?" Reagan's voice was strained.

Nerves raced like spiders across Sosimo's skin, and he glanced at Cooper standing in the entry. His eyebrows scrunched low over his eyes. He felt it too. Sosimo uncrossed his arms and straightened.

"Yeah. Such a shame to have your house ruined like that." Johnson spoke absentmindedly as he turned the suit over and over in his hands.

"But, I—" Reagan looked toward her father, who had sat forward in his chair, his nostrils flared.

"I never told you about her house." General Paxton's voice steeled as he scooted toward the edge of his seat.

Colonel Johnson's muscles tightened. "Now, this is a conundrum."

A chill raced down Sosimo's back and arms, turning his fingers cold. He took a step forward to grab Reagan. In a move that belied his age, Colonel Johnson grabbed her by the hair and pulled a pistol from his holster, letting the armored suit fall. She snatched the suit into her hands and bunched it in her grasp before it hit the ground. A screech of pain came from her that stood all of Sosimo's hair on end. Johnson pulled her up against him and placed the gun to her temple as Sosimo and Cooper trained their guns on him.

Her wide eyes met Sosimo's and held. That she sought him out and not her father settled the ringing and chaos scrambling his brain and focused him. He nodded at her, hoping the calm she'd given him somehow reflected back to her. Her gaze never left his as she twisted her hands in the Supersuit.

"What in the world—" Mrs. Paxton's exclamation ended with a shocked gasp as she stepped in from the kitchen.

"Hold it right there, Claire." Johnson tightened his grip on Reagan.

"Honey, go back into the kitchen." General Paxton stepped in front of his wife, blocking Johnson's view of her.

"No, Claire, I'd appreciate it if you'd stay in here. Take your husband's seat." The menacing tone ruined Colonel Johnson's polite words.

"Why?" Reagan shifted, but he yanked her back. "Why are you doing this?"

"Family, June, pure and simple." Johnson's eyes darted between Sosimo, Cooper, and the general. "I was told to help get your invention for some very powerful people. In exchange, they've promised to pay for alternative treatments for Lily. I didn't have a choice."

"I would've helped with Lily, would've paid for whatever she needed. You know that." The pain in Reagan's voice tore at Sosimo's heart. Everything she did was to help others and here one of her family's oldest friends hadn't even asked.

"It's not just about Lily." Another bead of sweat traced down Johnson's face as he adjusted his grip on the gun. "They'll kill Nancy if I don't. I can't lose my wife and my granddaughter."

"Do they have Nancy?" General Paxton asked, ignoring the choked sob that came from his wife seated behind him.

"No, but they don't need to have her in their custody." Johnson swallowed. "They're too powerful, Dan. Influence so much. I've seen how they force elected politicians to vote a certain way on bills or military personnel to make a command to their benefit. Their insidious reach is too long to fight."

"Commands in the military? How?" General Paxton's voice held indignation.

Johnson rolled his eyes. "There are several ways they've infected our military, but how about I give you a specific one?" He'd gained confidence, if the condescending tone showed anything. "What happens when a Special Ops team doesn't have all the equipment available to assess a situation, First Sergeant Rivas?"

Sosimo's stomach dropped to his toes. "The mission goes south."

"It's interesting how one call can make equipment disappear that would've not only saved the lives of comrades and innocent hostages but kept a supply of trafficked sex slaves hidden safely on the other side of the wall." Johnson's eyes hardened. "That's just one example in the South American jungle. There are thousands. There's no going against these people."

Sosimo's heart pounded loud in his ears as images of that last mission flashed through his mind. Hadn't Sosimo and his team questioned where the Superman device had gone? He blinked away his clouded vision, connecting with Reagan's gaze. The pain and anger he felt was mirrored in her eyes.

She jerked her head a fraction and mouthed "Ready?" No, not at all. Especially for some half-cocked plan that would get her shot. He answered with a quick shake of his head. She rolled her eyes and the corners of her lips lifted in a slight knowing smile.

"Enough." General Paxton's voice came out sharp. "What do you want?"

"The suit," Johnson answered. "And, unfortunately, I'll need June."

"How could you?" Mrs. Paxton's voice shook.

Sosimo didn't dare take his eyes off of Reagan. She started mouthing a countdown, and he steeled himself. He'd never had anxiety threaten to choke him. Then again, he'd never had the woman he loved trapped in the hands of a desperate man. He pushed the stifling fear down and focused all his energy on getting Reagan safe.

Three, two, one. She jerked her head back, cracking her skull against Johnson's nose, and twisted. As she fell, she reached for the gun. Sosimo roared as he jumped across the space. He tackled Johnson as a shot blasted in his ear. Reagan screamed, but Johnson's punch to Sosimo's ear had him fighting to suppress the enraged man. Cooper swung, his gun smashing against the colonel's face and knocking him out cold.

Silence settled on the room like a wet blanket. Sosimo turned to Reagan who knelt on the floor, her fingers tangled in the suit and pressed against her gut. No, she couldn't be shot. He scrambled, not able to get to her fast enough for his liking, and knelt in front of her. With shaking hands, he reached toward her, not wanting to see how bad the wound was. She opened her fingers, spreading the fabric wide, and dropped a bullet on the floor. His breath whooshed out in a sharp exhale.

He pushed the hair from her face. "You okay?" The words barely passed his lips.

She nodded, but before he could pull her to him, her mother dissolved into sobs and rushed to Reagan. It was better that way. He still wasn't sure what to do about him and Reagan. When all the trauma of today finished, the massive wall of mistrust would still be there. He stood, willing his shaking knees to straighten and not buckle.

He looked at Adam Johnson, who lay out cold on the floor, the man's words tumbling through Sosimo's brain. Hadn't they always felt that there was more to that mission? Deception had ripped Ethan Stryker from their lives. Had forever changed Jake when the bullet tore through his femoral artery and shattered his femur. Veiled truths had caused so much havoc in his life.

Could he have a relationship with someone who built their career on a lie? He shook his head. That was something he wasn't sure he could do.

FIFTEEN

June lay in bed, staring at the ceiling. The day played in her head on constant repeat, tormenting her with pain and indecision. The MPs had come and taken Adam away. The torment and tears that had streamed down his face as he'd apologized gripped her heart tightly.

In the morning, she'd set up a fund for whatever Lily needed for treatment. She rubbed her eyes that were dry and scratchy. She'd have to contact her banker, make sure only Lily could use the account. She groaned. Now she had to be paranoid about her accounts as well? When would it end?

She yanked the blankets off and got out of bed. She needed a cup of tea. Maybe her mom had a secret stash of Valium or something hidden behind the spices. June grabbed the sweater her mother had lent her and shook her head. She'd never take them even if she found some.

On silent feet, she descended the stairs. She paused as she entered the kitchen and her gaze caught a figure on the porch. Her throat closed while she scanned the kitchen for a weapon. The figure shifted, and the moonlight highlighted Sosimo's profile. Her knees gave out as the tension rushed from her, causing her to lean against the doorjamb for support.

Then just as quickly, her heart picked back up and her palms slicked with sweat. He'd avoided her the rest of the day. Granted, there had been a lot to take care of with Adam being arrested and their statements being taken. She'd just wanted to step into his arms and feel the strength of them around her. Keeping her gaze trained on him during the afternoon's fiasco had been the only thing holding her together. She'd seen the love she felt shining from his eyes toward her. She knew it. Now, it was like she had the plague.

She pushed the doubt aside and crossed the kitchen to the sliding door. He stiffened when she stepped outside but didn't turn to her. She swallowed, her throat suddenly a desert.

"Sosimo?" Her words were barely audible to her ears.

A slight breeze rustled the bare branches, the only sound as she waited for his answer. Time stretched as she leaned toward him, willing him to speak.

"June." He spoke her name in a short tone of indifference.

Icy fingers of dread slid down her spine. She wrapped her mother's sweater tighter around her, fully aware that the only arms holding her were her own. She took a tentative step forward.

She cleared her throat. "I've been wanting to talk to you."

"Cooper will stay on with you," he spoke at the same time.

"Wait, what?" She stumbled toward him.

"You no longer need two of us, especially if you stay here until you deliver the suit." His tone came out efficient, matter-of-fact, and drove a spike through her heart.

"Why don't you?" She hated how her voice shook.

"Can't."

Won't was more like it.

"I'm sorry ... I'm sorry I didn't tell you." She curled her toes against the cold, wooden deck and inhaled the autumn night air to calm the nausea threatening her throat. "It's just ... I've protected myself for so long ..."

His jaw clenched in the moonlight. What could she say that didn't add more insult to the wound? She should've told him long ago when her heart first started whispering its desire to be free from the lies. In everything but her name, she'd been more real with him than she had ever been with anyone else, even herself. Besides, she *was* Reagan. On some levels, at least. She squared her shoulders and took a step closer.

"We have something special between us. You know it. Please don't leave." Her voice cracked at the end, ruining her strong words.

His shoulders slumped and his head bowed, throwing his face into complete darkness. Hurt radiated off him, tightening her muscles in response. *Oh God, please.*

"You're right ... but you lied." He looked over at her then, his eyes filled with pain. "I don't even know you."

She shook her head as heat bloomed up her chest. "I didn't lie. I just didn't tell you everything."

"And there's a difference?" His laugh came out harsh.

"Reagan is my name now. Has been for years." She pointed at herself, trying desperately to control the anger surfacing. She didn't want to yell. She wanted him to see the truth. "And you want to know why? Because people only ever indulged me when my name was June because my father was the general."

She fisted her hands in her sleeves and peered into the dark forest that lined her parents' backyard. Her first proposal for her Superman invention came to mind. How the injustice of the day had set her on a course to her new life.

"When I was eighteen, I got the chance to propose my Eyes Beyond invention to the Defense Advanced Research Projects Agency. The project was still in its infancy, but I'd isolated enough of the problems to make it more than plausible." She did a quick shake of her head, not wanting to relive the next part. "I had paused outside the door, trying to collect myself, when I overheard the two men I was presenting to. One asked why they were indulging a pampered teen girl in the first place. What a waste of his time it was. The other reminded the man that if they sat through this meeting and nodded their heads, the general would put all his support and weight behind a new product they wanted to push out to the troops."

How those words had crushed her tender heart. Not to mention that her father hadn't thought her invention good enough on its own merit.

"Their vacant stares and well-timed nods told me they only sat through the meeting to appease my father.

When I asked my father, he said he was only trying to help." She crossed her arms to keep her hands still. Sosimo's firm stare turned away from her rising anger. "From that point on, I knew that the only way I wanted to make it was on my own, without what my father could do for someone influencing the decision. So I did what I needed to step out of his shadow."

She took one more step and jabbed Sosimo in the arm, pulling his focus to her. He rubbed his hand down his shirt and across his heart. She willed him to listen.

"I shared more of myself with you than I have with anyone ... ever. You know me, Sosimo." Her nose stung. Her anger bled away to desperation. "You know the real me."

He stared at her a long time, his gaze traveling every inch of her face. Seconds passed, allowing hope to float to the surface. She bit her lip as the weight of the tension of the last two weeks lifted. He shook his head, and the weight crashed back down.

"I have to go." He moved past her, angling so he wouldn't touch her. "Stay close to Cooper."

The click of the glass door as it slid close shattered her heart like a bullet to a glass bottle. She wobbled on liquid knees to the porch swing and collapsed on it. She didn't blame Sosimo, not really. How could she expect him to trust her? She pulled her knees to her chest and wrapped her sweater around her legs. As an engine started in the dead silence of night, she leaned her forehead onto her knees. The sound faded, leaving only the harsh knocking of empty branches against themselves. All her hopes for a future beyond the lonely life she'd locked herself in rushed down her face in salty streams of anguish.

SOSIMO LEANED on the railing to the dock as the sun faded in the sky, reflecting off the Potomac from light pink to dark purple. Lights from neighboring cottages blinked on up and down the river. Soon the sky would be dark, just like his mood. An owl hooted a long, mournful call, one Sosimo felt to the depth of his soul.

He was foolish to come back to the cottage June, Cooper, and he had rented that last night of their road trip. Foolish to spend every night of the last week staring over the black water. To sleep in the bed she had, imagining that the fruity smell of her candy still lingered. He had told Cooper and Zeke he wanted to stick close for a few days just in case Cooper needed help with anything. That had been a lie, making him the biggest hypocrite of all.

He grabbed onto the railing, gripping it with so much strength the wood bit into his skin. Good. Maybe the pain of his body would displace the pain in his heart. He growled and pushed away from the railing.

When his phone had rung an hour earlier, his stomach had leaped into his throat, hoping June was calling. Idiot. She would never call after the way she'd poured everything out to him and he'd left her without a word.

It'd just been Cooper letting him know she'd had a meeting with the SEP. They were excited, and everything was a go. Coop would stick around for one more night to escort her to a ball honoring the general. Apparently, she'd decided to go public with her connection to her father.

He didn't like how exposed her decision made her. Ironic how her coming forward as General Paxton's daughter had frozen the blood in his veins to ice. Her going public would only make her a bigger target. He scoffed. He wanted her to be honest with him, but not the world? Yep, he was an idiot.

He pushed his hands through his hair and let his head drop back. Staring blankly into the clouds that shifted over the moon, he thought back to that last night when he had closed his heart to her and walked away. The moonlight had highlighted all her yearnings she hadn't hidden from her expressions. He'd stared into her face, shining with such hope, almost stepping close to hold her. Then a cloud had blown across the moon and for a second shadowed her face and cloaked his heart in fear. Did he truly know her?

He closed his eyelids shut, and she filled his brain. Her talking to person after person about supporting soldiers while her palm trembled on his arm. How horrified she was when she'd put Eva in danger. Her tears when she'd despaired at not being able to protect Jake and Ethan.

He looked over the water with a huff. Other moments rushed to him every time he closed his eyes. He rubbed his hand across his chest. Man, he missed her.

She was right too. He knew her. She was more than a name. She was the woman who'd voiced deep yearnings of belonging when he'd described his rambunctious family. The desire to take her home to his madre swelled in his chest until he thought he'd suffocate.

"Suficiente!" he whispered to the ghosts. "Enough," he voiced more strongly.

Turning, he stomped back to the cottage. He'd already decided, foolish as it was. The decision bound him now, the consequences of his stupid pride.

SIXTEEN

Sosimo pulled away from the cottage, determined to put distance between him and his memories of June. He'd been indulgent to hang around and wallow in his grief. He just wanted to get home to Colorado and lick his wounds. Maybe some stressful jobs could help him forget the empty cavern where his heart had been. The more dangerous, the better.

He pulled onto the highway on his way to the airport, his mouth parched with the thought of being so far away from her. Zeke had a plane waiting for him at the airport. Sosimo couldn't get out of Virginia fast enough.

The phone rang. He flinched with the intrusion. Not wanting to stop when he'd just started, he clicked the answer button on the steering wheel without taking his eyes off the road.

"Yeah?" He flipped on his blinker to pass a slower car.

"Rivas, this is General Paxton."

Sosimo swerved, nearly running into the car next to

him. He waved as the car honked, accelerating to get around. His heart beat in his throat.

"Sir, is June okay?" Sosimo pulled onto the shoulder of the road and slammed on his brakes.

"No, soldier. She's not." The sharp words had Sosimo checking his side mirror to weave back into traffic and race to her. "Of course, she's not okay. Some imbecile broke her heart."

Sosimo rested his head on the steering wheel as relief relaxed his muscles. She wasn't in danger. Then why did he still want to rush to her?

"My intel tells me you're not doing so hot either."

He chuckled a humorless laugh and sat up. "Intel, huh?"

"Listen, son." The general's tone lost its bluster. "I know what my Junebug did was wrong. She should have told you earlier that she'd changed her name. It's my fault, really."

"How's that, sir?" Sosimo stared at the cars as they rushed by.

"Did she tell you about the young man who almost stole her Eyes Beyond invention?"

"Yes."

The general sighed long and low. "Did she tell you he was my assistant and that I pushed for her to accept his pursuit?"

"No, she didn't tell me that." A sinking feeling dropped Sosimo's stomach to the floorboard.

"She saw right through him before I did. My quiet little bug was even bold enough to confront me about it." General Paxton tsked.

The thought of June as a quiet bug made Sosimo's neck hot. He clenched his teeth to keep from snapping at the general. June may get away with it, but years of respecting the chain of command held his tongue.

"I brushed it off. Told her she just needed to get out of the lab more often and learn how to socialize." The general paused. "I can tell by your silence that you're upset."

Sosimo squeezed his hands around the steering wheel. "Yes, sir. June has more sense than anyone I know. And just because she's reserved, doesn't mean she's quiet. She's passionate and caring, bright like the sun shining hope on others." Ay, caraye. Way to leave your heart out there, Rivas.

The general chuckled low. "You're right, son. She's all that. Problem is, men only ever saw her as an extension of me. And me, being the numskull I am, never understood her. But I understand her now, and I think you do too."

"Sir?"

"Don't be a numskull, Rivas."

Sosimo sighed and knocked his head on the driver's seat. Hadn't he wanted to turn the vehicle around that night the instant he put it in drive? June deserved better than someone like him, someone who couldn't see beyond his own ego.

"Sir, it doesn't matter. I hurt her, walked away without saying more than a handful of words. Even if she would take me back, I don't deserve her."

"This is the problem with you Special Ops boys." Gen. Paxton sighed like Sosimo's madre did when one of her kids pushed her to her limit. "We train you to be self-sacrificing, to give up your life for another, but too often that carries into your life where you don't need it."

"I'm sorry, sir, I don't think I'm following." Had what little intelligence Sosimo had left with his heart?

"Son, you're willing to sacrifice your happiness because you think she deserves better, when what she deserves is you." The force of the General's words slammed Sosimo in the chest. "I've looked into you. You're an honorable man, Sosimo Rivas. I wish I had more soldiers like you under my command."

Sosimo's skin itched at the declaration. His entire life he had strived to be more than just the dumb gearhead who couldn't read and always got in trouble.

"But more than any of that, I saw the way my daughter's eyes went to you in that mess with Adam. Which, by the way, pinched like the devil. I saw the love and trust shining from her, never once doubting that you would save her." The general's voice dipped low. "I also saw your support for her, how you came to her defense against me even when you were upset with her. And the anguish on your face when you thought Adam had shot her."

Sosimo leaned his head back against the seat and closed his eyes. The intense pain of that moment churned in his gut again. He couldn't lose her.

"Son, I'm telling you, she'll take you back. If you're willing to put aside your pride and fear, that is."

"I hear you Lima Charlie."

"Finally. All this emotional mumbo-jumbo was making me itchy." The exasperation in General Paxton's voice made Sosimo smile. "Saddle up, Rivas. I've got a plan."

Sosimo nodded as he listened to the mission the general laid out. The wrenching pain that had lodged in his gut eased as the plan unfolded. Though this mission might not be riddled with gunshots and kidnapped diplomats, it was probably the most important one of all.

JUNE SAT at the table assigned to them for the dinner as the musicians played beautifully and attendees waltzed across the dance floor. She'd almost backed out of coming. The pride on her father's face as he'd introduced her around, proclaiming to all how his genius of a daughter would save so many lives, had been worth the discomfort and anxiety.

She'd reached her limit of interaction, though. Maybe she should've worn a sackcloth instead of letting her mom go shopping with her. This dress, while beautiful with its deep purple color and just enough exposed skin to still be conservative without being dowdy, had drawn too much attention. If one more man came up and sat next to her, regaling her for her beauty or smarts, she might just puke the expensive dinner she hadn't been able to taste all over them. While her father's pride in her had filled her heart with warmth, the bombardment of men eager to impress her, then chase their platitudes with questions of her father, made her wish she could escape to her lab. Too bad she had blown it up.

Her hands shook as she fiddled with the napkin in

her lap. She still hated these types of events, even after becoming Reagan, philanthropist extraordinaire. She'd only felt at ease during her charity event when Sosimo stood beside her.

She rolled her eyes at herself and tossed the napkin onto the table. There she went again. She needed to stop wallowing in her self-pity. She was starting to stink of it.

"Everything all right?" Cooper leaned close to ask quietly over the music.

"Yeah, fine."

Poor Cooper. Not only did he get stuck babysitting her all week, hanging out at her folks, twiddling his thumbs, but now he got stuck sitting here, bored out of his mind. She kept telling him to go ask the multitude of ladies that threw encouraging smiles his way to dance. Even made a point of picking out the ones she thought he'd look cute with. He'd just scoffed and shaken his head.

She didn't know what she'd do without his calm presence. While he had a great sense of humor, it was more quiet and teasing. Mostly, he had a patience that gave him the ability to be content in just about any situation. He'd sat with her for many hours this last week just staring at the bare trees.

Sitting on that porch, he'd shared about his own heartache, about coming home to find the woman he loved had married another. When she'd come to his defense, he'd claimed it was his own fault. They'd been friends forever, but he'd never told her how he felt. Said he had wanted to wait until he got out rather than to put her through being a Marine's wife. His story had given her hope that maybe she'd find some peace in the days and weeks to come. June had welcomed the camaraderie and prayed he found someone who appreciated the gift of him.

"Think it'd be all right to skip out now?" June looked around for her parents, hoping to catch their attention.

"Maybe. You stick here. I'll just step out in the hall and coordinate our retreat." His conspiring whisper and wink made her chuckle.

Almost the instant Cooper left, the seat on her other side filled, like the vulture had been circling for an opening. She felt his heat as he leaned close. Please, Cooper, hurry.

"It's not right that the most beautiful woman in the room is sitting alone." The deep, sultry voice froze the room.

Her heart pounded so hard in her chest she swore it'd pop out at any moment and land on the fancy tablecloth. Sosimo leaned toward her, his soft smile not hiding the wariness in his eyes. He inched closer, placing his hand on the back of her chair.

"Of course, if another man sat here, I might just lose it." His whisper blew across her neck and stood her hair to attention. He rubbed the back of his fingers across her exposed shoulder. "You look beautiful, cariña. Como una flor."

"Why are you here?"

She wanted to throw her arms around him and never let go, not ask stupid questions he probably wouldn't answer. She darted her eyes around, looking for Cooper.

He cleared his throat, drawing her attention back to

him. Not that it ever left. "I'm here to beg the most amazing woman in the world, the woman I love more than life itself, to forgive a fool too stupid for his own good."

She covered her mouth with her fingers as she shook her head. "You're not stupid." She blinked to keep the tears firmly behind her eyelids.

His eyes narrowed before he glanced around the room. "Can we find someplace to talk?"

She nodded, her voice blessedly deciding to not work. She couldn't trust what would come out at that exact moment. He ran his fingers down her arm, leaving a trail of fire in their wake, and clamped his hand tight within hers. He pulled her to her feet, then headed for the nearest exit. When her legs refused to move properly, he wrapped his arm around her waist and practically carried her out of the stifling room.

With him firmly pressed against her side, all the pain and uncertainty of the last week fell away. Had he really come back for her? She almost couldn't bear to hope, but the intensity of his expression and the soft words he'd spoken said he had. Air rushed into her lungs, leaving her lightheaded. He found a private alcove in the empty hall and tucked them into it.

Her legs wobbled at the sudden stop, but she steeled them. She didn't have time for weakness now. She closed the space between them, grabbed the back of his neck, and pulled him to her. She kissed him hard, full of the desperation and pain that had almost overwhelmed her. She wrapped her other arm around his shoulders and speared her fingers through his hair, drawing him closer.

Voices echoed down the hall, and he moved them farther into the dark of the alcove, pressing her against the wall, never leaving her mouth. Sparks of joy flew from her head to her toes. Her brain might short-circuit with the sudden change in emotion. He was here. Her brain could melt, for all she cared.

He pulled away and wrapped her in his arms, his face buried in her neck. He trembled as he pulled her closer.

"Please tell me your kisses mean you forgive me." His voice shuddered under her ear.

She loosened her death grip on his jacket and smoothed her hands up to his shoulders. "Only if you forgive me for not telling you who I am."

He cupped her cheek with his hand and rubbed his thumb along her jawline. "I've always known who you are." He took in all of her with his eyes, smoothing the back of his fingers down her cheek and neck. "You're June Paxton, champion of soldiers, beautiful introvert who downs chewy candy by the bagful, the most intelligent woman alive." He leaned forward and kissed under her ear. "You're the woman who's captured my heart, who challenges my thoughts, and makes me want to be better."

She flexed her finger and swallowed the lump stuck in her throat. "I'm not all that."

"You're right." He kissed her lightly on the lips. "You're so much more. You're the woman I want to marry, to take home to mi madre, to make redheaded babies with."

"Sosimo?"

"I know we haven't known each other long, but I

can't go another day without you, cariña. This last week just about killed me." He leaned his forehead on hers. "Marry me, please."

"Sí." She couldn't say more past the joy clogging her mouth.

"¿Sí?"

"Yes, Sosimo Rivas. I'll marry you, though your madre intimidates me a little."

He picked her up and whirled her around. The distant music picked up pace as if in celebration with them. How could life change from despair to everything she ever wanted in less than an hour? She squeezed him tightly as he placed her feet back on the floor.

"Don't worry. She's gonna love you. Could we have a small wedding and marry soon? I don't want to share the day with anyone but us and our parents." He ran his hands up her back.

"What about your friends and your siblings and all your family?"

He shook his head. "I don't want chaos at our wedding. Just you. They can all celebrate with us later."

"I like the sound of that."

"Great. I've got it all planned." Sosimo beamed as he pulled her toward the ballroom. "Let's go tell your parents."

He kept her mind whirling as he explained what he had arranged. It was crazy and impulsive and made her giddy with excitement. After filling her parents in, he held her close on the dance floor, swaying to the music long into the night, whether the tempo played fast or slow. It would have embarrassed June Paxton, making her want to hide from the knowing smiles and curious glances. But June-soon-to-be-Rivas no longer wanted to be the timid girl with sweaty palms and trembling hands any time she had to step from her lab. She was finally ready to firmly embrace who she'd become in Reagan, and with Sosimo by her side, her insecurities seemed to dissolve like sugar on the tongue.

SEVENTEEN

Sosimo paced at the end of the dock while he waited impatiently for June to join him. He still couldn't believe he had pulled off organizing the wedding in two days. They could've had it at her parents' place, but since Virginia didn't have a waiting period, Virginia was where the wedding would be.

He liked the fact that they would marry at sundown overlooking the Potomac. He paced back to the other side of the dock. If she didn't hurry, the sunset would be over.

"Man, you pace anymore and the end of the dock will fall off." Cooper chuckled from where he leaned at the railing, calm like always.

When Sosimo had found out that Cooper was a bonafide clergyman because of his baby sister wanting him to officiate at her wedding, he'd thought God had been smiling down on him. Now, he just wanted to push the infuriating man into the river. Since that would delay his wedding even longer, he contained the urge.

"Mijo, I'm so proud of you." His father, who had

arrived with Sosimo's mother the night before, threw his arms around Sosimo's shoulders, stopping his pacing. "You've done something special here for a special lady. I'm so glad to be a part of this."

His dad motioned at the dock. Sosimo took it all in again. It had been a lot of work transforming the humble dock into a place worthy of June's wedding, but it had been worth it.

His father, General Paxton, and Cooper had all helped him while the moms had gotten June ready. He'd lined the walkway from the cottage with pots of fall flowers in varying reds, pinks, and oranges that reminded him of the many shades in June's hair. They'd strung twinkling lights up and down the length of the dock from tall poles they'd attached to the pillars, ending at an arch of lights they'd stand under to exchange vows.

The hope was that she'd step out of the cottage when the sun displayed its best show across the sky and the ceremony would end with the sky darkening and lights twinkling overhead. The real hope was that she wouldn't regret not having a bigger wedding. They had covered the cottage windows facing the river with foil so she couldn't peek. According to a text his madre had sent, they'd had to pull June through the cottage door off the drive when her curiosity almost got the best of her. Now, if she would only hustle so he wouldn't ruin all this work by dragging her out here.

The cottage door opened and shut just as quickly. His heart leaped into his throat. His madre rushed down the dock, a huge smile across her face. His heart settled back where it belonged.

"She's ready. Get set, mijo." She kissed him quickly on the cheeks and shooed him to his spot.

He stepped up to the arch, wiping his sweaty palms on his pants. Cooper smirked as he tucked his Bible under his arm. Sosimo straightened his tie and turned toward the cottage.

His heart pounded in his throat as the door opened, and June walked out. He could tell the moment she took everything in by the way her shoulders tightened and her mouth dropped open. Her parents stepped up to both sides of her, and they escorted June down the dock to him.

Her gaze darted from one place to another until it zeroed in on him, never swaying the entire walk. The simple satin dress she'd bought that day perfectly draped over her and shimmered in the setting sun. She hadn't covered her hair with a veil. He loved the play of light in her wavy strands. She'd tucked some flowers from the vase he had left in the cottage around her head like a crown. She took his breath away.

When she took his hand and stepped up next to him, tears sparkled in her eyes. "This is perfect."

The ants tangoing in his stomach stopped when he threaded his fingers through hers. "I'm glad."

Cooper started in with his, "Dearly beloved," and Sosimo stared into June's eyes. Her fingers didn't tremble, and her smile shone confidently at him. As songbirds and the passing river serenaded their ceremony, years filled with love reflected in June's teary gaze.

THREE WEEKS LATER, June stared at the house as Sosimo pulled into the drive of his parents' house. She fanned her silk shirt, hoping her antiperspirant didn't fail her. She felt silly getting so dressed up with the beautiful top and calf-length skirt that flared when she spun. She'd hoped to make a good impression, but now was just uncomfortable.

Her father's voice came over the speakers of the car. "Son, thanks for the names of people to look into for the force I'm putting together to untangle this group Adam says controls the world or whatnot. Hopefully, we'll be able to tear the organization down to dust."

"I'm glad I could help, General." Sosimo put the car in park and turned off the ignition.

"Rivas, I've told you to stop calling me that."

Sosimo laughed. "Sorry, sir. Old habit."

"Right. I'll let you go. Tell your parents Claire and I say hello. Oh, and Junebug, keep that young man of yours in line."

"I will, Dad. Love you." She bent forward and stared at the bright curtains hanging in the windows of the house. "Is it too late to fly back to Zeke's island for a while longer?" She glanced at Sosimo, half hoping he'd say yes.

Their honeymoon had been amazing on the private island Zeke had inherited from his grandfather. No one but the food delivery guy from a neighboring island had been in that small piece of heaven. When she added her Latin hunk of a husband, who liked to whisper sweet words in Spanish, the island tempted her to never leave. As soon as this visit finished, she'd look into how to buy an island of her own.

"Cariña, it won't be that bad." He threaded his hand through hers and kissed her wedding ring. "Madre promised it'll be a small gathering today."

"Okay." June took in the calm he always settled over her.

He kissed her on the lips much too quickly for her liking and got out of the car. As he rounded the front, she checked her reflection in the mirror. She rolled her eyes at the lipstick on her teeth and wiped it with a vengeance as Sosimo opened her door and reached for her hand.

"Did I tell you I got a message from Zeke this morning?" He wrapped his arm around her waist and led her to the door.

"No."

She only remembered him coming into the room of their suite with his phone while she changed her outfit for the fifth time. One look at her and he had dropped his phone on the dresser, and, well ... her neck heated. She didn't need to think about that now. He peered down at her, a satisfied grin on his face.

She rolled her eyes. "What did he say?"

"They've started the renovations on the old manager's house at the ranch. There wasn't as much needed done on it as we thought, and the contractor thinks they'll be able to finish, lab and all, within three weeks."

"Really?"

June still couldn't believe Zeke wanted them to settle there. At first, she'd been hesitant, but the more she and Sosimo had talked about it, the more she saw the benefit. The lab would be more secure than if they found a place on their own, and he could still do the job he was made for—protecting those in need. While she'd never imagined herself married to a military man, she was humbled and proud of the man she called husband.

"Stop staring at me like that, or I may just drag you back to the hotel and disappoint my madre." Sosimo pulled her tighter to his side and kissed her.

"Would that be so bad?" she whispered on his lips.

He growled low and kissed her hard, just as the door opened and loud, rapid talking flooded the air.

"Mija! Mijo!" Sosimo's madre's voice pulled them apart. "Ay, caraye." She swatted Sosimo's arm while pushing him aside and threading her arm around June's waist. "Let the poor woman breathe."

June stifled a laugh as she smiled over Madre Rivas's head. Sosimo rolled his eyes and rubbed his arm. June squeezed her lips together to keep from snorting out a laugh.

"We just have a few of us here today. The rest will come for the party tomorrow." Madre Rivas patted June's side in a comforting move as they stepped through the door.

Chaos erupted as more people than she could count crowded around to hug and kiss both her and Sosimo. More names and rapid Spanish flew her way than she knew what to do with, but the warmth and love enveloped her in a cocoon of happiness.

When it seemed like the entire town had finally said their hellos and dispersed throughout the house and the back door, Sosimo wrapped his arm around her. "You all right?"

She placed her hands on his chest and smiled up at him. "Yeah. You're right. They're wonderful."

"I'm not sure if I ever said that." He scrunched his face up. "Annoying and overbearing, sí, but wonderful?"

She swatted him on the arm, gasping in shocked indignation and stepping toward the noise in the kitchen. "Careful, I'll tell Madre."

"No, anything but that." He grabbed her around the waist and pulled her back. "I'm glad you like them."

His kiss touched softly on her lips, like she was a cherished treasure. She finally felt found, that she didn't have to be so alone anymore. No more living behind lies and shadows. As Sosimo pulled her to join his family, she knew he would always be her home.

EPILOGUE

Three weeks later, June stared at the house as Sosimo pulled into the drive of his parents' house. She fanned her silk shirt, hoping her antiperspirant didn't fail her. She felt silly getting so dressed up with the beautiful top and calf-length skirt that flared when she spun. She'd hoped to make a good impression, but now was just uncomfortable.

Her father's voice came over the speakers of the car. "Son, thanks for the names of people to look into for the force I'm putting together to untangle this group Adam says controls the world or whatnot. Hopefully, we'll be able to tear the organization down to dust."

"I'm glad I could help, General." Sosimo put the car in park and turned off the ignition.

"Rivas, I've told you to stop calling me that."

Sosimo laughed. "Sorry, sir. Old habit."

"Right. I'll let you go. Tell your parents Claire and I say hello. Oh, and Junebug, keep that young man of yours in line."

"I will, Dad. Love you." She bent forward and stared at the bright curtains hanging in the windows of the house. "Is it too late to fly back to Zeke's island for a while longer?" She glanced at Sosimo, half hoping he'd say yes.

Their honeymoon had been amazing on the private island Zeke had inherited from his grandfather. No one but the food delivery guy from a neighboring island had been in that small piece of heaven. When she added her Latin hunk of a husband, who liked to whisper sweet words in Spanish, the island tempted her to never leave. As soon as this visit finished, she'd look into how to buy an island of her own.

"Cariña, it won't be that bad." He threaded his hand through hers and kissed her wedding ring. "Madre promised it'll be a small gathering today."

"Okay." June took in the calm he always settled over her.

He kissed her on the lips much too quickly for her liking and got out of the car. As he rounded the front, she checked her reflection in the mirror. She rolled her eyes at the lipstick on her teeth and wiped it with a vengeance as Sosimo opened her door and reached for her hand.

"Did I tell you I got a message from Zeke this morning?" He wrapped his arm around her waist and led her to the door.

"No."

She only remembered him coming into the room of their suite with his phone while she changed her outfit for the fifth time. One look at her and he had dropped his phone on the dresser, and, well ... her neck heated. She didn't need to think about that now. He peered down at her, a satisfied grin on his face.

She rolled her eyes. "What did he say?"

"They've started the renovations on the old manager's house at the ranch. There wasn't as much that needed done on it, and the contractor thinks they'll be able to finish, lab and all, within three weeks."

"Really?"

June still couldn't believe Zeke wanted them to settle there. At first, she'd been hesitant, but the more she and Sosimo had talked about it, the more she saw the benefit. The lab would be more secure than if they found a place on their own, and he could still do the job he was made for—protecting those in need. While she'd never imagined herself married to a military man, she was humbled and proud of the man she called husband.

"Stop staring at me like that, or I may just drag you back to the hotel and disappoint my madre." Sosimo pulled her tighter to his side and kissed her.

"Would that be so bad?" she whispered on his lips.

He growled low and kissed her hard, just as the door opened and loud, rapid talking flooded the air.

"Mija! Mijo!" Sosimo's madre's voice pulled them apart. "Ay, caraye." She swatted Sosimo's arm while pushing him aside and threading her arm around June's waist. "Let the poor woman breathe."

June stifled a laugh as she smiled over Madre Rivas's head. Sosimo rolled his eyes and rubbed his arm. June squeezed her lips together to keep from snorting out a laugh.

"We just have a few of us here today. The rest will

come for the party tomorrow." Madre Rivas patted June's side in a comforting move as they stepped through the door.

Chaos erupted as more people than she could count crowded around to hug and kiss both her and Sosimo. More names and rapid Spanish flew her way than she knew what to do with, but the warmth and love enveloped her in a cocoon of happiness.

When it seemed like the entire town had finally said their hellos and dispersed throughout the house and the back door, Sosimo wrapped his arm around her. "You all right?"

She placed her hands on his chest and smiled up at him. "Yeah. You're right. They're wonderful."

"I'm not sure if I ever said that." He scrunched his face up. "Annoying and overbearing, sí, but wonderful?"

She swatted him on the arm, gasping in shocked indignation and stepping toward the noise in the kitchen. "Careful, I'll tell Madre."

"No, anything but that." He grabbed her around the waist and pulled her back. "I'm glad you like them."

His kiss touched softly on her lips, like she was a cherished treasure. She finally felt found, that she didn't have to be so alone anymore. No more living behind lies and shadows. As Sosimo pulled her to join his family, she knew he would always be her home.

Don't miss *Celebrating Tina*, the next book in the Stryker Security Force series.

A K-9 handler determined to prove she belongs. A detective with an unwavering plan. Can they overcome their painful pasts and accept the gift of love?

Tina West has spent her life feeling like she stood on the outside, but since taking a job at Stryker Security, life seems to be turning for the better.

Tina never imagined when she took a job as a nanny she'd end up training for search and rescue. Yet, when her boss shows up with a retired military dog and the opportunity to train with him, Tina snatches up the chance to help those who are lost. If she saves enough people, maybe she could find meaning in a life that left her with nothing but a bruised heart and a tarnished picture of family. As holiday festivities loom before her, she wonders if she'll ever shuck the regrets that haunt her dreams and keep her from connecting with others.

Milo Bishop's every move has been to take care of his mom and younger brother.

Since his father's murder, Milo has worked hard to make sure his mom and brother were provided for. He joined the police force straight out of high school, took night classes so he could move up to investigator, and put his life on hold until his brother graduated from college. But when he is rescued on Thanksgiving Day by Tina West, his well-laid plans take a sharp detour.

When a series of kidnappings threaten to ruin the holidays, can Tina and Milo put aside their doubts and find the abducted children before it's too late?

ALSO BY SARA BLACKARD

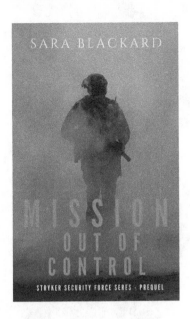

SARA BLACKARD

MISSION
OUT OF
CONTROL

STRYKER SECURITY FORCE SERES · PREQUEL

It was a mission like any other ... until it blew apart around them.

When the Army's Special Ops team is tasked with infiltrating the Columbian jungle and rescuing a kidnapped State Department family, the mission seems like every other one they've executed. But as the assignment unravels, not only is the mission's success at stake, but all the brothers-in-arms leaving the jungle alive hangs in the balance.

Mission Out of Control is the prequel short story for both Vestige in Hope and the Stryker Security Force Series.

www.sarablackard.com

ABOUT THE AUTHOR

Sara Blackard has been a writer since she was able to hold a pencil. When she's not crafting wild adventures and sweet romances, she's homeschooling her five children, keeping their off-grid house running, or enjoying the Alaskan lifestyle she and her husband love.

CPSIA information can be obtained
at www.ICGtesting.com
Printed in the USA
LVHW091319211220
674518LV00012B/321